ALSO BY DEBBIE BOEK

If Not For The Knight
Knights Are Forever series
Book #1

When The Knight Falls
Knights Are Forever series
Book #2

Winter's Knight
Knights Are Forever series
Book #3

Sommers' Folly

THE DEVEREAUX CHRONICLES

Devil's Bait

Devil's Retribution

Devil's Gathering

Devil's Veil

Visit the author at:
debbieboek.com

This story is dedicated to all of you that continue to accompany the Devereaux' on their various adventures.

DEVIL'S JUBILEE

Book #5 of the Devereaux Chronicles

Debbie Boek

Copyright © 2020 Debra Boek

Wolf Rider Publishing

All rights reserved.

Paperback ISBN: 1-7342482-3-8
ISBN-13: 978-1-7342482-3-4
Ebook ISBN: 1-7342482-4-6
ISBN-13: 978-1-7342482-4-1

CHAPTER 1

Lying on the floor where she'd been tossed, Annie Kincaid's hazel eyes opened wide as she struggled to comprehend what she was seeing.

The evening had started out like many that she and her boyfriend, Jason, had shared over the last few months. The two of them were sitting close to each other on the tattered old couch in his tiny apartment. They were completely caught up in a silly horror flick playing on the television when all hell broke loose and the horror suddenly became real.

The front door burst open with a loud bang that startled the both of them. It hit the wall so hard that some of the hinges were dislodged, leaving it hanging at an awkward angle as a stranger burst through the doorway.

He was an older man wearing a wool hunting coat and holding a deadly looking pistol in his hand. Annie barely had time to notice those items when Jason leapt up from the couch.

Before Annie even knew what was happening, and with a strength that she didn't realize he possessed, Jason picked her up and threw her across the room, out of the line of sight of the muzzle of the gun which was now pointed directly at them.

Annie hit the wall hard and slid down, dazed but still conscious. She covered her ears to mute the sound of the gunshots reverberating in the small room. Everything was happening so quickly that she could barely process it.

In such close quarters, it was almost unbelievable that Jason wasn't fatally wounded by a bullet, but he weaved and ducked quicker than the eye could follow as he crossed the room towards the stranger.

The man tried to keep the gun trained on Jason as he moved about and quickly emptied the clip, with little results to show for it.

Blood started to seep through Jason's shirt in two different spots, but the wounds didn't seem to faze him at all as he relentlessly continued forward.

Annie watched in bewilderment, not sure of what, if anything, she should do. Jason no longer looked like himself, he seemed to be changing into something else before her very eyes; his arms were now longer, animal-like nails grew out from the tips of his fingers and the snarl he let loose was definitely not human.

With one swipe, he left a trail of deep gouges along the man's face, barely missing one of his eyes. Blood started spurting everywhere and the stranger screamed and stumbled backward.

Jason slowly moved in on the man, who was now defenseless and cowering against the wall, using both of his hands to try and staunch the flow of blood from the deep lacerations on his cheek, but he couldn't contain it all as it continued to ooze through his fingers.

Now that his screams had faded, the sound of approaching sirens could be heard. Jason took another step towards the stranger and raised his hand again, ready to finish him off.

Annie watched as droplets of blood fell from his nails onto the ugly tan carpet. She must have let out some sort of noise because Jason paused and turned in her direction. His lips were pulled back, showing his teeth and his eyes, which were always an unusual amber color, and which now seemed to almost glow in the lamplight.

They sought her out and he stared long and hard at Annie, as if he wanted to communicate something, but no words came from his mouth.

Instead, he snarled one more time, cocked his head to gauge how close the police cars were, then took off out through the broken door and into the darkness of the night.

Annie slumped further down onto the floor and tried to wrap her head around what had just happened, ignoring the moans coming from the stranger across the room as he continued to try and stop the flow of blood from his wounds.

"I understand if you'd rather not go, Scott. I'm just throwing it out there," Tim added, seeing the hesitation on his brother's face.

"I don't want to leave you on your own, it's just that Emma could go into labor anytime."

Scott was struggling with indecision. He didn't want to send his brother off into potential danger all by himself, yet he couldn't leave Emma alone right now, either.

He strode over to the coffee maker and topped off his cup while he tried to resolve the matter in his own mind.

"Rufus is still there, just a little banged up. He and I can work this one. Emma needs you. Priorities, brother. It's not a problem."

Their eyes met in mutual understanding, but Scott still needed some additional reassurance.

"You sure you'll be alright? Rufus is no spring chicken, you can't expect him to have your back like I would."

"I'll be fine," Tim replied, then smiled. "Actually, I'll probably be much better than you will when Emma goes into labor. You just keep me posted, alright?"

"I will and if there is anything you need, call."

"Will do."

"What was that about?" Emma asked, just as Tim was closing the door behind him after he headed out. She made her way slowly over to the kitchen table and eased her body down onto one of the chairs.

"Tim caught a case in upstate New York."

"I thought you two were on hiatus?"

Tim and Scott Devereaux were hunters of all things supernatural or cryptid. They'd been doing so for many years after learning the trade from their father. With Scott's recent marriage to Emma and their first child together due any day now, the two brothers had agreed to hold off on any new cases until at least after the approaching Christmas holidays.

"We are, but a hunter we know, Rufus Downey, got cut up pretty bad and could use a hand with a situation."

"What kind of situation?"

"Not sure. Nathan called Tim to let him know about it, but he didn't have all the details."

Nathan Michaels and his wife, Polly, are the information epicenter for the few paranormal hunters that operate across the United States.

Tim and Scott, as well as the other hunters, relied on them for a multitude of things, not the least of which included notifications of any potential cases in their general vicinity, if they hadn't picked up on them already.

"Are you going to go help, also?"

"No," Scott said softly, seeing the worry in her brilliant green eyes. "I have my own issues to deal with right here. When is that little devil going to show his face, anyway?"

"It won't be long now, I'm pretty confident of that," Emma replied, running her hands over her extended belly and frowning as she tried, unsuccessfully, to get comfortable.

Scott brushed a long, blonde lock of hair away from her face and tried to hide his own nervousness. Emma had three other children from her first marriage, but this was all new to him and he did not like the feeling of helplessness that consumed him whenever he thought of her actually having to give birth.

"Do you feel alright? Do you need anything?"

"I'm fine." As hard as he tried, Scott could never hide the way he felt from Emma. She opened her mouth to reassure him, but a little squeal came out instead when the back door opened suddenly and a cold gust of air blew Gabriel into the kitchen.

"There you are," he said. "Just wanted to let you know the tree is up in the Great Room and Hannah and I are heading home to see my mom. Is there anything else you need first?"

They'd met the scrawny young man earlier this year during an adventurous stay in New Hampshire and had hired him on to help out at their newly purchased Bed and Breakfast. His girlfriend, Hannah, although painfully shy, was a wizard in the kitchen and they'd hired her on as a cook and housekeeper.

The Bed and Breakfast wouldn't be opened up until early spring, but Gabriel and Hannah had moved into an apartment a few miles away and were already on Scott and Emma's payroll.

"Get over here and give me a hug."

He looked down at his wet boots, shrugged his shoulders and tried to tiptoe the few feet between them, then bent down to give Emma a quick hug, as requested.

His faded red hair was long and wild, and Emma had to brush the errant strands from her eyes as she returned his embrace.

"Drive safe and give your mother our best," she said, once he'd released her and tried to step lightly back towards the door.

"I will, thanks, and good luck with the baby. We'll only be gone about a week so if you want to wait till then to have it, that might be better."

"I'll give that some consideration," Emma replied with a smile.

Scott stood up and walked over to shake his hand. "Enjoy your trip and your visit with your mom. See you soon."

"You sure you can handle this place?"

"Somehow, I'll figure it out, Gabriel."

After he'd escorted Gabriel out and shut and locked the door securely, Scott turned back to his bride with a mischievous smile.

"Do you hear that?"

"What?" she asked with a frown.

"That, my dear, is the sound silence, it's just you and me until the little guy decides to join us."

"Better appreciate it now, because when it changes, it's really going to change. I hope you're ready for how different your life is about to become."

"I'm ready and I'm actually getting a bit impatient. I do so hate waiting."

"Be careful what you wish for," Emma replied with a secretive little smile.

"What exactly did you tell the cops?" Tim asked.

He was sitting in a small motel room with Rufus Downey, who had thick white bandages taped to his left cheek to protect the torn skin underneath them. However, some blood had managed to seep through and Tim found the rusty stains on the bandages distracting while he tried to have a conversation with the man.

"I said that I heard a woman screaming so I kicked down the door."

"Did you?"

"Naw, I'd been following the guy and knew that was his apartment. But, I did not know he had a girl with him, never expected that. It knocked me for a loop when I first went in and saw her. I completely lost the edge I had over him."

"I assume she denied screaming to the cops?"

"Yes, but she was in shock from what I could tell and said very little to them or anyone else." Rufus scratched the scraggly hair on his chin.

"Cops ended up assuming I heard something on the TV, from some stupid movie they were watching."

"Did they press charges against you? For the gun?"

"Not yet, any potential charges are pending. And I got a license for the gun so that isn't a big deal, although letting loose inside an apartment complex might be."

There was a rakish smirk on his face as he continued.

"I think they are still trying to put together what they're dealing with. I was very vague about our fight. Said he cut me with a knife, didn't bother telling them he was changing into an animal and dug me with his claws. After all, I'm not ready to be fitted with my white jacket just yet.

Right now, I don't think they know if they should arrest me or him. After all, I'm an ex-cop and was just being a Good Samaritan."

"By letting loose a full clip in a tiny apartment? I don't understand how you didn't kill both of them," Tim said with a raised eyebrow, his expression emphasizing how implausible he thought the Good Samaritan defense was.

"Understood, but still, the shifter's actions look much worse than mine and it's really messing up the cops' theories."

"Have they found him yet?"

"Naw, he's MIA, and I don't think he'll be back to these parts. If the cops don't find him, I think I'm good with them. They are much more suspicious of him because he took off like that."

"Didn't the girl rat you out to the cops?"

"No," he said, rubbing his chin again. "I mean, she confirmed that I broke in, but that's all really. I know she saw it start changing and I'm wondering if that's why she kept quiet about everything that happened once I got inside. That or she thinks she's going crazy."

"So, what do you need me here for?"

"I want to stay under the cops' radar, but I think we might be able to get some info from her now that a little time has passed. I don't know if she's a shifter too but, at the least, she may have some info on where he is or where he might have gone."

"How many has he killed around here?"

"At least four."

"Why would he keep this girl alive if she isn't a shifter?"

"I did run that by Nathan, and he said they will sometimes collect a member of the opposite sex and breed with them."

"Part-shifter, part-human babies?" Tim asked with a shudder.

"That's what Nathan said, gives them cover, too. Helps them fit in with humans when they look like a normal family."

"Does the human involved know?"

"No idea. What do you say? Can you help me out with the girl? Like I said, she's seems traumatized and I don't think she'd react well to seeing me again."

"Sure, I can handle that for you."

Tim finally located the girl, Annie Kincaid, at the hospital a few hours later. Based on the information that he managed to get out of a pretty, young nurse on the floor, Annie had some minor injuries, but they'd kept her overnight due to the severity of the shock that she suffered.

Annie Kincaid was somewhere in her early thirties from what Tim could estimate, she was dressed and getting ready to leave when he reached her room.

Annie was still overwhelmed about all she'd been through and was moving around in a kind of a daze. She was startled when she turned and saw Tim Devereaux standing in her doorway.

Her heart started beating rapidly in her chest and she raised a shaking hand to her cheek to brush away a lock of curly brown hair as they quietly studied each other.

He was very tall and broad, almost completely filling the doorway. He was a handsome man, with strong facial features and his brown hair was grown out enough to frame his face and hide in the collar of his coat.

His soft brown eyes were lit with curiosity when he finally spoke. "Excuse me, are you Annie Kincaid?"

"I am, who are you?"

"My name is Tim Devereaux and I just have a couple of questions for you."

She looked at him quietly, her heart still hammering in her chest. "I have nothing to say about any of this, to anyone."

The police had taken her statement and she had not been completely honest with them, she couldn't tell them that her boyfriend had suddenly sprouted claws and began to change into some kind of animal. Instead, she just explained to them that Jason was startled at the intrusion and attacked the other man in self-defense.

What surprised and worried Annie the most was that the cops almost seemed more suspicious of Jason than of the intruder, simply because he took off after the incident and they still hadn't been able to locate him.

"It's very important that I get some information from you," Tim said. His voice was soft but firm.

A nurse pushed past him just then with a wheelchair.

"You're all checked out," she said. "I called a cab and they'll be waiting for you downstairs."

"I don't need this," Annie said, feeling silly and weak already, just by having had to stay overnight at the hospital.

"Please, I just have to take you downstairs. I have others to attend to and have no time to argue with you about it."

"You're busy, can I take her down?"

The young nurse looked harried and exhausted. She turned her wrist and checked her watch, then met Tim's eyes. "I could get in a lot of trouble but, if you wouldn't mind, it would really help me out. Just leave the wheelchair in the lobby."

"But," Annie said, before Tim cut her off.

"No problem, go take care of your other patients."

"Thanks."

The nurse hurried off and Tim pushed the wheelchair over closer to Annie. He smiled encouragingly and indicated she should take a seat.

Annie hesitated and then, with a clenched jaw, she released a frustrated snort of air through her nose, grabbed her purse and sat down heavily in the wheelchair without saying another word, draping her heavy wool coat over her lap.

"Please, don't worry," Tim said, as he pushed her out of the room and down the hall towards the elevators. "I promise that I won't hurt you, I just want to talk for a minute."

The elevator arrived but he held off on any further conversation as a half dozen other people crowded on to it with them.

When they reached the first floor, Tim bent over her shoulder and asked, "Can I give you a lift home or do you want me to take you out front to the cab?"

Annie was filled with indecision. To the left was a hallway leading to the parking garage and to the right was the front entrance of the hospital. She gasped loudly when she glanced over towards the front doors.

"What's wrong?" Tim asked, sensing her sudden anxiety.

"Is your vehicle in the parking garage?"

"Yes."

"Good, take me there, quickly, please."

He glanced over towards the glass doors and saw a tall, swarthy man coming through them. He was carrying a bouquet of flowers and his attention was completely focused on them as he tried to save the petals from being crushed by the jostling crowd entering the building alongside him.

Tim pushed her down the hallway, trying not to move too fast and bring any unwanted attention their way, as he swerved around others headed slowly in the same direction.

He was fairly certain that the tall, swarthy man never noticed the two of them.

Annie stood up just before they reached the doors leading to the parking garage. She was still a little dizzy and had to grab hold of Tim's muscular forearm as she tried to regain her balance. He wrapped his arm around her to keep her upright and led her into the garage.

His truck was parked on the lower level and he kept his arm around her as they hurried down the incline towards it. Quickly unlocking the doors, he helped Annie up onto the passenger seat and then went around and climbed in himself.

"Was that your boyfriend?"

"Who?" she asked, feigning ignorance.

"The tall, dark man who was coming in through the front doors."

Annie slid her gaze his way, trying to decide what, if anything, she would share with him.

"Who are you and why are you interested in what happened to me?"

"My name,"

"I know, your name is Tim Devereaux, but who the hell are you?"

Now it was Tim's turn to decide how much information to share with her. Blowing out a deep breath, he thought it would be best to be as honest as possible with her, maybe he could gain her trust and she would open up and share the details of what had happened and how they could find the shifter.

He was obviously still in town, but Tim couldn't confront him here, especially not with Annie here, as well. But, she might know where he was hiding out.

Assuming, of course, that she was not also a shape-shifter. If so, she wouldn't share a damn thing with him, which would be telling all in itself.

"I'm a hunter. I hunt paranormal creatures, as does my friend, Rufus Downey, the man who broke in on you and your boyfriend last night."

Annie's hand snaked over to the door handle.

"Please, don't. Obviously, you didn't want your boyfriend to see you. I can protect you from him."

"I don't need protection," she said, but her voice was low and unsure.

"I think you do. Jason Turnbull is your boyfriend, right?"

"Yes." She had tears in her beautiful hazel eyes and Tim knew she was still feeling overwhelmed and confused about the entire ordeal.

"I won't do anything that you don't want me to. Can I start the truck and get us out of here?"

She hesitated and he watched her closely. The chance that she might also be a shifter seemed like a long-shot. If Annie was a shifter, then she was also an excellent actress because she truly seemed traumatized and unsure of herself, of him, and of everything that was happening.

"He's in the hospital looking for you right now. I would strongly suggest we get away from here, and soon."

Her breath caught in her chest. "Yes, let's get out of here, but I can't go to my apartment. He knows where I live."

"We'll stop somewhere for a cup of coffee and I'll answer all your questions and, hopefully, you'll answer mine. Then we can decide what to do next. Is that alright?"

"Yes, please hurry," she whispered, turning her head to stare towards the door leading from the garage into the hospital.

CHAPTER 2

"Exactly how bored are you with all of this?" Emma asked, wrapping her arms around Scott's neck and leaning heavily against him. His dark brown eyes were softer than normal as he gazed down at her.

"I'm not bored at all. This has been fun," he said, brushing her hair back from her cheek before leaning down to gently kiss her lips.

They had just finished putting the changing table together and now the nursery was complete. Scott glanced around the room, feeling proud of what they had accomplished with her creativity and his brawn.

It was a good-sized room but there was minimal furniture in it; a crib, changing table, dresser and the obligatory wooden rocking chair with a cushioned seat over near the large window.

One wall was completely covered with a mural of a dozen or so cartoonish zoo animals with a woodsy background. Above the changing table were a half dozen pictures of baby animals, each with their own positive affirmation.

Scott knew it would be years before his son or daughter would understand why the baby giraffe was encouraging them to stand tall or why the lion cub was letting them know that they should be brave, but one day all of them would come mean something to his child.

"Bam," he said, pulling back away from Emma and resting his palm on her extended stomach, "that kid can kick."

"Tell me about it, I think he is even more bored than you are. He wants out."

Scott and Emma decided not to confirm the sex of the baby via the ultrasounds, but both of them usually referred to the unborn child as a boy and, because they couldn't be absolutely sure, they went with the animal theme which would be appropriate for either sex.

"I'm not bored, seriously. If I seem like that, I think it's more that I'm a little unsure. He's going to be here any day now and that reality is beyond exciting, and yet, also completely terrifying."

Emma smiled and ran her fingers along his tense jawline, the tips of them rubbing the scruffy beard he'd been growing for the last couple of weeks.

"I think that beard makes you look even more ruggedly handsome. You're going to keep it for awhile, aren't you?"

"Depends on the next job we get. When we have to play parts it usually works out better if we're clean-cut. We look more trust-worthy that way, but I'll keep it for awhile, just for you. Christmas is only a few weeks away, maybe I'll even play Santa."

Emma burst out laughing.

"What's so funny about that?"

"That is so not your style. Although, you have been a lot more patient with my kids the last couple of months, so maybe that could work."

"When are they coming, anyway?"

Emma had three children from her previous marriage, her two sons, James, age fifteen, and Collin, who was almost seventeen, went to a boarding school and had been spending most of their free time living with their father, Jeremy Draper.

Her daughter, Shelly, was a college student and lived in an apartment about a half an hour away.

Now that they had purchased a home of their own, Emma was hoping that her children would spend much more of their time here. And since this was their first Christmas altogether, Emma wanted it to be perfect.

"I guess that depends on this guy," she said, rubbing her stomach. "Jeremy is ready for the boys to come here as soon as possible. He and his little girlfriend, Lori, are taking a Christmas ski vacation somewhere out west.

It would be great if this fellow would make his appearance soon and give me a few days to recover before they arrive but, regardless of my situation, Shelly is picking them up some time the end of next week and the boys will be staying until after the first of the year when their classes begin again."

"And what about Shelly, is she going to stay here for awhile, too?"

"I hope so, at least until after Christmas, but who knows. She's a little unpredictable lately."

"Lately?" he asked, with one brow raised.

"More so than usual."

"That sounds more like it. Are we done in here? It looks good."

Scott glanced around the room one last time. It was a warm, comfortable room and, hopefully, all the furniture they recently assembled would stay in one piece once they actually had a chance to put it to use.

Lifting an eyebrow as he turned towards his wife, Scott said, "Did we really need the ginormous stuffed giraffe over in the corner?"

Emma couldn't hide her smile as she shrugged her shoulders. "It was on sale, I couldn't resist."

He shook his head and rolled his eyes, but his face became more serious when he said, "You did great job with this room. I can picture you sitting over there, snuggling up in that rocking chair with the little nipper."

A wistful smile appeared on his face that made Emma love him even more than she already did, which she hadn't thought was possible.

"We're all set now," she replied softly, glancing around the room and feeling a great sense of peacefulness come over her. The last few days she'd been almost manic, trying to get everything in order for the holidays and for the baby's arrival, but now she felt calm and ready.

"Why don't you go down and start lunch. I'll just fold up the last of these clothes and put them away."

"Sure," he replied, giving her a quick kiss before walking out to the kitchen.

The sprawling, old farmhouse had been semi-converted over the last few months in anticipation of opening it up as a Bed and Breakfast at some point early the next year.

Their personal quarters took up most of the first floor and no guests would have access to that area.

Only a few rooms in the front of the house would be available for the guests to use. The large staircase was just inside the front door and off to the side of it was a large, cavernous Great Room, or the Good Room, as Scott usually called it.

There were shelves filled with books, DVDs, games and cards available should the guests choose to avail themselves of them in front of the large screen TV or the roaring fireplace.

Right now, there was a large, full Blue Spruce standing bare in front of the bay window. Scott thought it looked a little silly but, although Emma made the entire rest of the room, and a great deal of the other parts of the house, look very festive with garland and lights and more Christmas decorations than Scott had ever seen, she insisted that they wait until her kids arrive to decorate the tree.

Some traditions could not be altered and that was a special time that she always spent with her children and which she treasured.

The only other rooms on the first floor that would be available to the guests would be the half bath under the stairs in the foyer and the dining room next to the Great Room where breakfast would be served.

The second floor held five large bedrooms, complete with their own shower stall and bathroom, and a small sitting area at the top of the stairs.

Since no guests would be there at this time, the empty rooms would be used by Emma's children. Tim and his mother were free to stay in the extra rooms, as well, if they chose to stay over.

Scott was thinking about his mother as he sliced tomatoes for their sandwiches. He suspected that she might want to take advantage of those vacant rooms once the baby arrived.

He couldn't help smiling at the thought of how animated and excited she was about having her first grandchild make an appearance. It was heart-warming to witness and surprising, because he'd never realized how important that would be to her.

Scott's hand froze in place when he suddenly heard Emma frantically calling his name. "Holy shit, it's time."

There was an awkward silence after the waitress brought their coffee and Tim couldn't put his finger on why he felt so keyed up. There was something about Annie that put him off his game and left him feeling a little unsure of himself.

He raised his warm brown eyes and studied her as she slowly stirred more sugar into her coffee. She was a petit woman with delicate features that emphasized her natural beauty.

She kept her eyes downward, which gave Tim an opportunity to study her a little closer. His gaze wandered over the soft brown curls that floated around her head, the high cheekbones and the unblemished porcelain skin.

Annie appeared to be slight and fragile, but there was a reticence and inner strength about her which intrigued him and made him even more curious about who she really was.

"So," Tim said, tired of the uncomfortable silence between them, "tell me about yourself."

Lifting her hazel eyes to meet his, she said, "Why?"

Tim shrugged his shoulders. "I thought this might be easier if we got to know each other a little better first."

"What exactly is 'this'? I don't even know why I'm sitting here with you. Especially when every instinct in my body is telling me to head out and get as far away from this town as I possibly can."

"I get that. You just went through a terrifying experience and I think that would be anyone's initial reaction."

Her hand shook a little as she raised her coffee cup to her lips. Setting it gently back down onto the saucer, she met his eyes once more.

Annie's eyes were hazel and they easily captured Tim's attention. In the short amount of time that the two of them had spent together, her eyes had already changed several times.

Usually they were a soft brown color but, they could also have more of a green tint or even a brilliant golden hue, depending on the lighting. They could change in an instant, reflecting her mood or her thoughts.

Tim could also see the suspicion in them but didn't know how to reassure her. He decided his best bet was to be as truthful as possible and hope she could wrap her brain around what he told her.

"There are two things that you have to tell me before I will even consider answering your questions."

"What are they?"

Annie didn't respond immediately because the waitress returned to their table just then.

"Would you like a little more coffee?" she asked, glancing back and forth between them.

"No, thank you," Tim replied.

Annie never took her eyes off Tim's face, just placed her hand over the mouth of her cup and waited for the waitress to move along to the next table.

When she did, Annie spoke softly, "Tell me what your interest is in what happened and what will you do with any information that I give you?"

"I'm a hunter and your boyfriend is the type of creature that I hunt. He is a danger to people in general and I need to help rid the world of him and his kind."

It was a rather blunt statement, but Tim knew of no way to sugarcoat those particular facts.

"What do you mean, his kind? And what do you mean, rid the world of him? Do you plan on killing him? That's why that man broke in last night, isn't it? To kill Jason?"

There were deep lines across her forehead and a vein throbbed in her neck as she tried to take in everything that was happening and process the crazy information that he was sharing.

"Listen," Tim said, reaching across the table to take her hand in his. "I know this all seems very unbelievable, but I'm being completely honest with you. He isn't a human being and we can't let him continue to kill people."

"Who is he killing? What people are you talking about?" Her voice raised a few octaves and several people turned to stare at them. Annie didn't even notice but pulled her hands out of

Tim's grasp and stared into his eyes. "And you didn't answer my question."

"Yes, that's why Rufus was there. None of this is coming out right," Tim said, shaking his head in frustration. "Let me try to explain a little better. I think your boyfriend, what's his name again?"

"Jason."

"Jason, right, we believe that he is responsible for some recent deaths here in town. Whatever information you can provide will help Rufus and me track him down, so we can prevent him from doing it again."

"Why not let the police take care of it?"

"It's complicated."

"Then uncomplicate it because I'm not telling you anything until I'm a lot more comfortable with your explanation and your plan."

"You saw him start to turn, didn't you?"

"I don't know what you're talking about," she replied, but looked back down into her cup, unwilling to meet his gaze.

"Yes, you do. He's a shape-shifter. You saw him start to turn and you know he is not a human-being. That is why you feel so traumatized about what happened, because you can't accept what you saw."

"I don't even know what a shape-shifter is or what I saw. I do believe that I imagined some details because they couldn't possibly have happened the way that I remember them."

"Yes, they could and that's why I'm here. To stop it from happening again. You are afraid of him now, aren't you?"

She nodded her head.

"Deep down, you know what you saw. And you know it was not natural."

"I thought he was turning into a werewolf and that I was losing my mind," she whispered, as a teardrop fell onto the Formica tabletop.

Tim looked around the diner, making sure no one was listening in to their unusual conversation.

"It was something like that, do you know where he might have gone?"

Her eyes met his and the lines across her forehead were even deeper now.

"Even if I knew, I wouldn't tell you, not if you plan on killing him."

"You aren't safe, you realize that, don't you?"

"No, I really don't. He's never done anything to me, Jason has never even raised his voice in anger."

"Why are you so frightened then?"

"Because I did see what was happening, and I can't put that together with the Jason that I know."

"That's kind of my point, he's a creature, he's not the Jason that you thought you knew. And he can't have a witness that knows the truth about him. Obviously, he's been able to hide what he really is from you, at least until last night.

You have to trust me on this. Do you have somewhere that you can go where he can't find you? Someplace that he doesn't know about?"

"My only family is my grandmother. She lives in Maine, but he knows all about her because she raised me."

"Damn," Tim said, thoughts spinning in his head as to how he could best keep Annie safe. He couldn't leave her unprotected but if they stayed in this town, the shifter would easily be able to track her down.

"My brother and his wife own a B&B in Pennsylvania. It isn't open just yet, but they can put you up until we're sure that you'll be safe. Would you mind going there until we can get this straightened out?"

"But I have a job and I have a life here."

"He can't let you live and you have to get that through your head. You'll have to give up what you have here, at least for now, until we are able to take care of him permanently. Otherwise, you'll never be safe again."

"This is all so surreal. I can't even grasp that it's truly happening." She ran her fingers absently through her hair and Tim could see the vein throbbing in her throat.

"He was my damned boyfriend, how could he be some kind of a monster? How could I not know that?"

"He's spent his entire life hiding what he is, and you certainly would have had no reason to suspect what he really is. Give yourself a break, there is no way you could have known."

"So, why should I trust you? For all I know, you might be some kind of a monster, too."

"True, but I'm not. I can't prove it to you one way or the other, you are just going to have to take my word for it and trust your gut."

"Of course, because that's worked out so well for me so far, right?" Annie stared hard at him, the green tint in her eyes hardening into little shards of ice as she struggled to make up her mind.

The soft brown curls swirled around her face and Tim's fingers itched to reach out and bury themselves within it. Annie was an enigma, so strong, yet so fragile at the same time. Tim desperately hoped she would agree to go to Scott and Emma's because he wanted more time with her, time to learn what made her tick and time to explore the feelings that were blossoming within him.

"You want me to hop back into your truck and go to some place in Pennsylvania with you. And trust that you aren't a serial killer that's going to murder me along the way?"

"Pretty much," Tim replied with a mischievous smile.

"That's not even close to funny."

"I know," Tim said, the grin widening on his face. "I understand your concern, but I am no serial killer and you're just going have to trust me on that."

"I'm not sure I can."

Tim opened his mouth to respond but closed it abruptly as his eyes slid over to his phone and he read the text that just came in. His grin widened even further and there was an excited glint in his eye when he turned his attention back towards Annie.

"Listen, my sister-in-law just left for the hospital. She's having my brother's baby and I need to get back there. I'm just going to lay my cards on the table. You have to choose what you want to do. I'm not going to force you into anything."

"What do you mean?"

"I can get you out of this town and keep you safe until we take care of Jason. You can stay at the B&B and you should be fine. If you don't feel comfortable with me, which I do understand, you'll have to stay here and take care of yourself. You'll be on your own with no one to watch out for you.

If Jason wants to protect what he is, he'll be visiting you real soon and I don't think you'll live through the experience. Your call, do we go pack you a bag and head out, or do I drop you off and leave you to deal with him yourself?"

Annie was quiet for a moment as she agonized over what she should do but, looking at Tim, she decided her best move for now would be to stay with him.

"I wish I wasn't such a fan of horror movies because I feel like I'm about to make a really stupid move." She was twisting her hands together in her lap and the vein in her neck was throbbing wildly. "Let's get my stuff and I'll go with you, but what about my job and my apartment?"

"We'll deal with that later. Let's just get you safe for now."

Tim parked two blocks away from her apartment building and left Annie slunk down in the passenger seat.

"He'll be watching for you, so keep your head down and I'll be back as soon as I can."

"But won't he see you?"

"It's an apartment building, he doesn't know me and won't know who I'm going to see. I'll be fine."

He returned about fifteen minutes later and threw the packed suitcase into the backseat of the truck.

"I hope I got everything. If not, we can pick up whatever you need when we get to Pennsylvania."

"Why are you doing this? I understand the hunting part but, why are you going out of your way for me like this?"

Tim took his hand away from the key and stared out through the windshield. Then he turned to Annie, and said, "It's what we do, we help people."

It was difficult to read the look on her face, to Tim it seemed to be disbelief and skepticism, and he could only hope that one day he'd get to know Annie well enough to find out what horrors she had been through that made it so hard for her to believe that someone might only want to reach out and help her, without having any ulterior motives.

CHAPTER 3

By the time that Tim and Annie arrived at the hospital, the baby had already been delivered. Emma was snuggling him close to her chest when they entered the room.

Scott was sitting over near the window, his face was pale and he looked completely drained, and yet, there was glow of happiness in his eyes that Tim could not ever recall seeing before.

His mom, Doris was there, as well, and she frowned at him. "Family only, Tim. Who is this?"

"I'm sorry, this is Annie Kincaid, I'll explain everything later. Can I meet the new family member first?"

Emma lowered the red faced baby and smiled warmly at Tim. "Meet your nephew, Brian John Devereaux."

Tim was not an overtly emotional person but suddenly found himself blinking back tears. "After my dad?"

"Yes, your dad, Brian, and my father, John. What do you think of him? Isn't he beautiful?"

"Would you be offended if I said he looked like a miniature Yoda? And what's with all that hair? Is that normal?"

"Of course, some are born with lots of hair, some not so much." Emma's voice was slower and quieter than usual, and Scott could see that she was exhausted.

"Thank you for coming," Scott said, nodding his head towards the doorway in a not too subtle fashion. "I think Emma might need a little rest right now. I'll walk you downstairs."

They couldn't talk much until they got to the lobby because of the crowds of people around. Once there, Doris made it her business to stick around and hear Tim's explanation about the girl.

"Annie, this is my brother, Scott, and my mom, Doris Devereaux." He turned to Scott with a challenging gaze.

"Rufus was hunting a shifter, who it turns out was dating Annie. She didn't know," he added quickly. "Rufus went after the shifter when they were together and Annie saw him start to change. So far, neither Rufus nor I have been able to catch up with it and I couldn't leave her alone.

He'll be trying to silence Annie and she has nowhere else to go. I thought maybe we could put her up at your place until we get the shifter thing straightened out."

Doris stood back, watching Annie while Tim explained what had happened. She was a pretty young thing and stuck close to Tim's side, apparently trying to use him as a shield against the rest of the world.

But it was the expression on Annie's face that most caught Doris' attention. Her eyes were narrowed as she stared at Scott and her lips were pressed flat in frustration and angst. Doris was not sure quite what to make of the young woman.

"Tim, walk with me for a minute," Scott said. He'd also noticed the looks that Annie was throwing in his direction, but they were not his main concern at this point.

The two of them stepped down the crowded hallway and left the women standing uncomfortably near the front doors.

"We aren't even going to be home for a day or two and when we do go back, we're going to have a brand-new baby with us. I don't want a stranger living in my house under those circumstances."

"I get that, but I had no other choice. I can't leave her back there. He'll kill her, Scott. You know he will. Rufus is still on the hunt for him. Hopefully, by the end of the week the situation will be resolved and she can go back to her own life."

"What do you know about her?"

"Not much, I just met her today and we saw the shifter, Jason Turnbull, show up at the hospital and I had to get her out of there fast."

"Why didn't you off him right then?"

"In the middle of a crowded hospital?"

"You had the bait that you needed to get him somewhere else."

"Silly me, I was thinking of her as a person, Scott, not as bait, so I guess I screwed up."

Scott blew out a long breath, he was still a jangle of nerves from witnessing his wife giving birth earlier in the day and was having a little difficulty dealing with this particular situation.

He ran his fingers roughly through his hair and was frowning when he met his brother's eyes.

Tim could see that he was wavering and felt he needed to push him just a little in the right direction. After all, it meant a great deal to him that they somehow keep Annie safe. He wasn't sure why, but he felt the need to keep her close by until he could be sure no harm would come to her.

"How about she and I both stay there? I was supposed to anyway, right? To take care of Callie until you two, I mean you three, get home."

"Right."

"You'll be staying here, won't you?"

"I'll probably go home to sleep tonight but come right back tomorrow. She could get released tomorrow night or they might keep her until the following morning."

"Okay, so let me get Annie set up there for tonight, at least, and we'll take it day by day until it gets straightened out. Maybe she can even help Emma out once she gets home."

"Why doesn't she stay at Mom's?"

"I considered that but, with the baby and then the holidays, we'll all be spending a lot more time over at your place. Not for nothing, but we can keep a closer eye on her if we're all there together."

"Christmas is over two weeks away."

"I know, that's a worst-case scenario. Rufus will catch up with the shifter well before then. But I'm throwing it out there just in case."

Scott glanced back down the hallway where his mother was making small talk with the young woman. Neither of them looked comfortable and Annie kept glancing down the hall towards them, and even Scott could see the look of quiet desperation on her face.

"It doesn't feel like I have much choice so she can stay for a few days. But, Tim, when I say she goes, then she goes, no questions asked. I will not let anything upset Emma right now."

"I get it and I don't want that either. You have my word."

"Here we are," Tim said, as they pulled up outside Scott and Emma's home.

As always, Annie kept her thoughts to herself when she got out of the truck and looked around. There was a good-sized lawn which was covered with a dusting of snow and beyond that a thick covering of evergreen trees.

The house itself was large and, although it was not yet dark outside, with the heavy clouds as a backdrop it looked almost forbidding.

Annie glanced over at Tim who was fiddling with the keys on his keychain, trying to find the one for the house as he headed up onto the wide porch.

She hurried along behind him and then waited until he found the correct key, inserted it into the lock and swung the door open to allow her to enter.

Annie was pleasantly surprised at how warm and welcoming the house was once you got inside. The large foyer was decorated with Christmas paraphernalia, garland was draped over the doorways and around the banister leading upstairs and poinsettia plants were scattered intermittently along the small hallway.

"All of the extra bedrooms are upstairs," Tim said, breaking her reverie as she tried to get her bearings. "Each one has its own bathroom and you can take whichever one you want. Hey, girl, what's the matter?"

Callie, Emma's German Shepherd, had come down the hallway to greet them but, as she got closer, she slowed down, then came to a full stop. The hair on her back was now standing on end and a low growl emanated from her chest as she stared at Annie.

"Keep it away from me," Annie said quietly, as she stepped back behind Tim, using him as a shield between her and the dog.

Tim was frowning as he moved forward towards Callie.

"What's up, girl? It's me," he said, ruffling her black fur as Annie sidled around him and took a couple of steps up the stairway, peering over the banister at them.

"I've never seen her greet anyone like that. She is getting older and maybe she's doing it because Scott and Emma aren't home. You don't have to worry about her, though, Annie. She won't bite you."

He hesitated when the low growling continued and Callie refused to look away from Annie.

"I have to run home and get some of my things. Why don't you go pick out a room and relax upstairs, do whatever you need to. I'll only be gone a half hour or so."

"What about that dog?" she asked, and Tim could see the beads of sweat above her lips, which trembled slightly with fear.

"I'll lock her up in the other part of the house until I get back."

"She won't be able to come up here?"

"No, I promise."

Tim watched Annie hurry up the stairs with her suitcase and felt another wave of protectiveness run over him. She seemed so small, so helpless and overwhelmed by the world, and the incident with Callie was just another example of how fragile she was.

He'd read that animals tended to focus on and attack the weakest of any species. Since weakness invites aggression, Tim that might explain why Callie had the reaction that she did. And maybe that's why the shifter had chosen Annie, as well.

Her situation resonated with Tim and, whatever it was that seemed to draw bad things to her, he wanted to change that pattern, to prevent anything bad from ever entering her life again.

Maybe, once they dispatched the shifter, he'd even take the chance that he'd been avoiding his entire adult life and see if he couldn't manage to have an actual relationship.

Annie brought out feelings in him that he wasn't used to, and he felt a strong need to take her under his wing and keep her safe.

In general, he'd always been an altruistic person and had devoted his life to helping others. But the way he felt now was different, primal and deep, and it seemed to get stronger with each minute that spent with Annie Kincaid.

"Are you sure you don't mind?" Scott asked. He was laying on the bed with his arm wrapped around Emma. She was cuddling their sleeping son against her chest and he was pretty sure that he would never feel so completely content again.

"It's fine, Annie needs help and we should be there for her. There's no danger in letting her stay, is there?"

"I don't believe so. The shifter would have no way of knowing where she is and Rufus is still on his tail. He's an experienced hunter and should have that resolved soon."

"Will he let you know when it's done?"

"Of course, Tim's been in touch to let him know we have the girl here."

The baby started fussing and she began to rock him gently in her arms until he quieted, unable to take her eyes off of him.

"How do you feel, Emma?"

"I'm really, really tired, but I don't want to close my eyes. I feel so peaceful and blessed, and I want to enjoy this quiet time with just the three of us."

Amazingly, the hustle and bustle and clatter of the patients, visitors and staff as they passed outside Emma's room could have been happening in a completely different dimension for all the impact that it had on the comfortable trio.

They were secure and happy in their own little cocoon, relishing every second and able to ignore everything outside of their immediate realm.

Scott reached his other hand up and brushed a lock of blonde hair from Emma's face, then kissed her forehead when she lifted her beautiful green eyes towards his.

"Can you believe that we haven't even been together for a full year yet? It's pretty incredible considering what we've been through and where we are right now," Scott said. His voice was low and raspy, and he realized that he was almost as exhausted as Emma.

"Surreal is about the only word that comes to mind when I think of where I was this time last year. Since then, let's see, we've taken on Bigfoot, bootleggers, a witch, a black ghost dog, and a bunch of other ghosts, to name just a few. I can't even imagine what next year will bring."

"In all honesty, even though Tim and I deal with those types of creatures all the time, they don't generally impact our personal life so, hopefully, the creatures still to be dealt with won't come visiting like they did this past year."

"Scott, sometimes, I do get very frightened. I didn't before, but now we have Brian, and the other kids will be with us occasionally. How do we make sure we are keeping them all safe?"

"We live life the same way we always have. You can't worry constantly about something coming for you, but you also can't bury your head in the sand and pretend the danger isn't out there somewhere.

We will stay vigilant and prepared, but life is not worth living if you are in a constant state of fear about what might happen. I'm here, Emma, and I won't let anything happen to you, to Brian, or to any other member of our family."

Emma snuggled in a little closer to his side, feeling reassured and safe, and it wasn't long before she gave in completely and lost her battle to stay awake.

"I thought you were coming back last night." Tim said, after Scott poured him a cup of coffee and sat down at the table in the little breakfast nook beside him.

A smile crossed Scott's face and he stretched his arms above his head. "I fell asleep on the bed with Emma."

"So, what does it feel like?"

"What?"

"Being a dad, what do you think?"

"Hard to say, the first thing that comes to mind is that I feel even."

"Even? What does that mean?"

"I guess that I finally understand what 'on an even keel' means. I'm just in a good place. Life is peaceful, the way it should be.

It's different than anything I'm used to. Don't get me wrong, I've always had a good life, it's just better now, complete."

Tim lifted the milk carton and poured a little into his Santa cup, staring mindlessly as the white stream swirled through his coffee while he slowly stirred it.

"You aren't losing your edge, are you?" Tim asked, raising his eyes to meet his brother's.

"Nope," Scott replied, not taking any offense at the question. "In fact, I feel even sharper and more focused. I guess I know what I'm fighting for now."

Tim didn't respond and had push away the little shards of jealousy that were attacking him because he wasn't able to experience those feelings himself.

"What's wrong, Callie?" Scott asked, as the dog rose up from under the table with a low growl.

He set his cup on the table and his face lost its dreamy expression as he stared across the room at the entryway into the kitchen.

Tim's head had also swiveled in that direction and he let out a loud breath of relief when he saw that Annie was peeking her head around the corner.

"What's the matter, Annie? You can come and join us."

Her small, nervous voice came eerily from around the corner. "I'm afraid of the dog."

The two men stared down at Callie, she had always been protective, but never aggressive, and listening to her low growl continue as the hair along her back stood on end, they both realized how out of character that behavior was.

"Come here, Callie," Scott said, a worried frown on his face. He led her to the back door and sent her on her way, then closed the door tightly and leaned against it. His face was tense as he tried to understand what could be causing Callie's behavior.

By the time he returned to the table, Tim had already coaxed Annie over and was grabbing her a cup of coffee.

"I'm sorry about that," Scott said. "Callie doesn't normally respond to people like she did. I take it you aren't a dog person."

The golden highlights in her narrowed eyes flashed as she stared at Scott, then she shook her head and turned towards Tim, reaching out to take the cup of coffee he was offering. Her expression immediately softened as she stared at the colorful Christmas scene on it.

"Emma goes all out for the holiday," Scott said, noting the look on her face. "I've been finding decorations all over, sometimes in the most unlikely places."

He rolled his eyes but couldn't keep the smile off his face. Annie appreciated the change in subject and decided to let Scott off the hook for his accusatory tone of voice while talking about the stupid dog.

"It's adorable," she replied softly, turning the cup around in both hands to take in the entire scene.

"Milk or sugar?" Tim asked.

"Just a little sugar, thank you."

"Any word from Rufus?" Scott asked, watching Annie closely as she stared down into in her cup, avoiding his eyes. She'd obviously just woken up and her dark curls swirled crazily around her head.

"Not yet, I'm going to check in with him later this morning if I don't hear anything."

"Would you two mind explaining to me what's happening and how long I'll have to stay here?"

"Well, I think we already talked about the fact that Jason is most likely a shape-shifter and that he won't want you to be around as a witness to that," Tim replied.

"Why not? As I told you before," she said, her voice was low but firm, "he has never been threatening to me in any way."

"He's a monster," Scott said, and Annie turned towards him once again, her face set and tense, an angry vein throbbing in her throat. "He needs to be put down before he hurts anyone else."

"How do you know that he's hurt anyone?"

"We don't know that firsthand, but our friend, Rufus, was following the bodies, and that's what led him to Jason. He can't be allowed to continue hunting humans. Once he's been stopped, you'll be safe and can return to your life. What do you do for a living anyway?"

"I work in a dentist's office," she said, then her eyes opened wide and her lips pursed in frustration. "I almost forgot, I have to call in and let them know I'll be gone for a little while."

She stood up to walk away, but then stopped and looked down at Tim.

"You forgot my charger for my phone and it's dead. Can I borrow yours to call in?"

"Sure, here you go. And don't tell them where you are or what's going on, alright? He may be checking in there, as well, to try and track you down."

Annie looked undecided but finally relented and nodded her head. She took the phone from his hand and wandered out into the foyer for a little privacy.

"You feel one hundred percent okay with her?" Scott asked.

"Yes, why, do you sense some sort of problem?"

"I'm not sure, something about her seems off and I really don't like Callie's reaction to her. I trust that dog's instincts more than my own."

"Give me a break, Scott. The dog is old and a stranger is in her house, that's certainly not enough to convince me there is some sort of an issue with Annie."

"Maybe not."

Scott shrugged his shoulders and took another sip of coffee as he mulled over the situation. He was willing to give Annie the benefit of the doubt, but he'd also be keeping a close eye on the woman until he was confident that Tim was correct.

CHAPTER 4

After Scott left for the hospital, Tim decided to drive Annie into the nearby town of Edgewater, so that she could pick up another charger for her phone and whatever other items she needed.

She played everything close to her chest and didn't talk much at all, but her face lit up when they drove into town.

It was a quaint village and truly came alive for the holidays. The storefronts were brightly decorated and Dickens' characters walked the streets, engaging with visitors and gathering together periodically to belt out a few Christmas carols or play out a few scenes.

Horses pulled carriages along the streets, decorated with ribbons and bells, and bringing to mind visions of Victorian Christmases past.

The sun was shining which helped negate the cold temperatures and, fortunately, there was no snow in the air and very little on the frozen ground.

"What a lovely place," Annie said, unable to stop smiling as she looked around.

"It is," Tim replied, enjoying the happiness on her face, which was usually so closed and secretive. He pulled into a corner parking lot and grabbed one of the last few available spots.

"I'm glad you like it. Let's walk around and you tell me where you want to go and what you'd like to see."

"Thank you for this," she replied, and moved over close beside him as they started down the sidewalk.

She giggled at the performers that they passed and there was a sparkle in her eye as she took in all the beautiful decorations. Shy at first, she became a little bolder as they continued around the village and, after a little time had passed, she would even grab hold of Tim's hand and lead him into the various stores that caught her attention.

He wasn't much for shopping but waited patiently as she looked over the items that she thought she might need, and then he pulled out his credit card and assured her that she could get anything she wanted.

In one specialty shop, Annie looked wistfully at a ceramic black cat, she turned it around and around in her hand and Tim could see it was something she genuinely liked. He encouraged her to get it, but she refused.

"Thank you, anyway, but I wouldn't ask you to do that. There is very little that I actually need, and this is just a frivolous item that caught my eye."

She reluctantly set it down and wandered towards the back of the store. Tim hastily set the cat next to the register and pulled out his wallet. The cashier wrapped it for him and, because it was so small, he was able to hide it in the inner pocket of his coat before Annie even knew that he'd purchased it.

Tim wasn't sure why he felt compelled to do that, but the holidays were fast approaching and, although her situation should be resolved by Christmas, they couldn't be sure of that. If not, it would make him happy to have a little something for her to open on Christmas morning since she would not be around any of her own family.

Once they'd gotten all the items that Annie thought she would need and threw them in the truck, he took her hand and led her towards the pond where the kids were ice-skating.

They stood close together along the rail, their arms touching comfortably as they laughed at the wipeouts and near calamities while they sipped their hot chocolate. For all the years that Tim had lived in the area, he'd never once spent the day like this and thoroughly enjoyed his afternoon with Annie.

Maybe it was because Tim was so relaxed in her company, or maybe because there were so many people bustling around them but, whatever the reason, Tim never noticed that someone had been following along and watching their every move.

Scott ended up spending that night at the hospital, as well, and both he and Emma were excited to take their baby home the following morning.

As soon as they entered the house, Emma couldn't help reflecting on what a difference it was from the peacefulness of their quiet hospital room.

She could ignore the goings-on in the hospital corridors, but not the commotion in her own home.

Callie was the first to hurry out and greet them, her tail whipping wildly back and forth as she got caught up in the excitement of their homecoming. She wasn't sure what it was all about, but there was a something in Emma's arms that had an unusual smell that she couldn't wait to check out a little closer.

Callie raised her nose toward the little bundle, but stopped suddenly as another smell overpowered its scent, and she turned and let out a low growl when Annie came downstairs to greet Emma and Scott.

"What's that about?" Emma asked.

"I think Annie's afraid of dogs and, for some reason, she rubs Callie the wrong way."

"Well, we'd better keep them apart, I don't want anything bad to happen. Callie's older now and she has to get adjusted to the baby, too. I don't want her to get all crazy on us."

Emma was quite perplexed because Callie had seemed perfectly fine, even with the new baby, right up until Annie came down to join them. Goosebumps rose on her arms as she stared at the attractive young woman, and Emma couldn't help but wonder if letting her stay with them was not such a good idea, after all.

Annie hesitated about halfway down the stairs. "I just want to thank you for letting me stay here. I really appreciate it and I'll try not to be a burden."

"You're welcome," Emma replied. And before she could say anything more, Annie glared at Callie, then turned and walked back upstairs to her room.

Tim helped bring in everything from the car and Emma wandered into their bedroom and set the baby down in the cradle that Scott's dad had hand-carved for him many, many years before. Doris had generously given it to them after having it restored.

For the time being, Brian would be spending the night in their room and having the cradle worked out perfectly.

They'd barely gotten the baby fed and back to sleep before Doris pulled in with Tolstoy, her seven-month old shepherd mix. He was still a crazy puppy with energy to spare and Doris left him outside to run around and burn off some of it before allowing him into the house.

She'd brought over a crockpot full of stew and some freshly baked biscuits so none of them would have to worry about cooking, for today at least.

Emma put Callie outside with Tolstoy, Scott and Tim set the kitchen table and, a few minutes later they were all enjoying their feast. Tim had trouble convincing Annie to join them until he made sure she realized both dogs were outside and wouldn't bother her.

Annie sat quietly and took small bites of the stew as the conversation went on around her, most of it about the baby. She did start to pay a little closer attention, however, when the conversation changed to talk about Jason.

"Rufus called earlier. He lost the shifter completely, thinks he skipped town. He is going to try and do a sweep of the nearby towns for a sign he might be trolling there, but he didn't sound hopeful."

"What does that mean for me?" Annie asked, looking up into Tim's soft brown eyes.

"Nothing just yet. We need to give Rufus a little more time."

"How much more and what is Jason exactly? You've given me bits and pieces of information, but I would appreciate it if you could break it down, give me the actual details about Jason. All that I really know, is that you think he's a killer."

She seemed agitated, which made sense since she had no idea of what kind of creature Jason actually was, or of the damage that he could do.

"We think that he's a shape-shifter."

"You've said that before, but it means nothing to me."

Scott was about to stab a piece of beef but stopped and set his fork down into the large bowl sitting in front of him. "A shape-shifter is actually a supernatural figure that can assume different forms."

"Werewolves?" Annie asked.

"That's possible, the lore goes back centuries, all across the world, and the most popular creatures in folklore everywhere have been vampires and werewolves."

"Shifting into the shape of a wolf is called lyncanthropy," Tim added, allowing Scott a chance to try his stew. "The old English word for man is 'were' and that is how the term werewolf came about."

"But," Annie's eyes were wide with confusion and Emma felt sorry for her. She, more than any of the others, could understand the complete tailspin that your mind goes through when faced with proof that creatures you'd always believed only existed in fairy-tales were, in fact, real.

"But," Annie repeated, trying to form her thoughts, "Jason and I dated for three months and he never changed into one of those, not even when there was a full moon."

"A full moon isn't necessarily required, a shifter can change any time, day or night, and they don't just change into wolves, they can become any living creature. Usually it's some sort of animal, but it can also turn into a person, which is what Jason must have done."

Annie made an attempt to eat some more stew but shuddered and set her spoon down. "What was he though? Was he human at all? We spent a lot of time together, how can any of this be real?"

"No one knows what they were originally," Scott said. He'd tried the stew and now wanted more, but reluctantly set his fork down once again, as he continued with the explanations.

"Shifters can be created in different ways, either through demonic manipulation, shamanism, sorcery or spells."

"Witches again?" Emma asked, and Scott could hear the tremor of fear in her voice.

"Not necessarily." He reached over and took her hand in his, gripping it securely.

"The Navajo call them skin-walkers," Tim added. "In their culture, skin-walkers are a type of harmful witch who has the ability to turn into, possess or disguise themselves as an animal. Or they can also inherit the ability."

"You mean shifters can have babies together?" Doris asked.

"According to the lore, yes, they can. And, apparently, they can breed with a human, as well."

"Oh, my God," Annie whispered, realizing what could have happened between her and Jason. "But, wouldn't there be something that would give them away? Wouldn't I have eventually realized that he wasn't human?"

"It's hard to say," Tim said. "There is still a lot that we don't know about them, there are very elusive and even hunters rarely have direct contact with them. From what I understand, they can freely change into any type of animal but, in order for them to transform into a human, they must first have something with that person's DNA.

Without the DNA, I don't believe they can complete the transformation, so he must have taken over someone else's body and that's why you had no way of knowing he wasn't a human."

"Is that why we have doppelgangers? Because a shifter stole someone's DNA and created another version of that person?" Doris asked.

"I'm not an expert," Tim said reluctantly, "but from what I've read, the DNA they take kills the human."

All of the women turned to stare at him, and Tim shrugged his shoulders.

"The lore is different depending on the part of the world it comes from but, the common consensus is that they have to ingest one of the human's organs in order to complete the transformation."

"That's disgusting and I find it hard to believe that such a vile creature truly exists," Emma said, standing up and leaving half her bowl of stew uneaten. "I'm going to go check on Brian. I'll leave you guys to finish your scintillating conversation without me."

Scott watched her walk away, his brow furrowed in concern.

"Damn," he mumbled, "we shouldn't have brought this up now."

"She'll be alright," Doris said. "I'll go talk to her."

"Why is your wife upset? Shouldn't I be the one that's in a tizzy about this?"

Scott didn't appreciate her tone or her implication. "You go ahead and dive right into your tizzy, Annie, but my wife just had a baby and has enough on her mind. She didn't need to hear all this shifter shit to give her something else to worry about right now."

Tim could read the look on Scott's face and decided it would be prudent to jump into the conversation and play interference before it got uglier.

"Annie, I know this has to be overwhelming for you, also. It's not easy to wrap your head around this kind of information. Are you okay? Do you have any other questions?"

Her eyes were narrowed as she watched Scott, up until then the only strong emotion that Tim had seen her exhibit was fear, but the look she threw at Scott was cold and calculated, and he realized that there was still much that they did not know about this woman.

Annie slowly turned to meet Tim's eyes, and her face relaxed as she let go of some of the tension that she was feeling.

She gave him a slight smile and lowered her eyes.

"Thanks, Tim, but I think that's about all the information that I can handle right now. I still can't believe that I didn't know. I have a history of poor choices in the man department, but this time I really outdid myself."

"You couldn't have known, don't beat yourself up about it."

"I think I'll go up to my room and try to let all this craziness soak in. It really is hard to accept."

"Let me know if you need anything," Tim said.

"I will, thanks." Annie never even bothered to look in Scott's direction as she walked out of the room.

"I don't think she likes me," Scott said, with a contemplative look on his face.

A knot was starting to form in his stomach as he watched her leave the room. Scott wasn't sure what it was about her, but there was something that was unsettling him, both physically and mentally, whenever she was around. And it was significant enough that he couldn't ignore it.

"Probably can't blame her," Tim replied, completely oblivious to his brother's concerns. He glanced around the now empty kitchen and asked. "You washing or drying?"

Doris entered the master bedroom and saw Emma staring down at her son in his cradle. She sidled up next to her and couldn't keep the smile from her face as she gazed down at his pure, innocent beauty.

"He looks just like Scott did. Have I given you those baby pictures yet?"

"Yes, you did, and I think you're right. This boy is going to look just like his daddy. He'll be a heartbreaker, that's for sure."

Emma reached her arm around Doris' waist and together they just quietly watched Brian sleep. It had taken some time before the two of them were able to set aside the past and their own bad feelings towards one another but, once they'd decided to do so, they had become very close, very quickly.

"What do you think of Annie?" Doris asked.

"I'm not sure," Emma replied honestly. "I feel bad for her and know this must be overwhelming but, in a way, I'm feeling a little selfish. We have a new addition to the family, my kids will be here in a few days and then we'll be spending our first Christmas all together. I was so excited about it, but now, she's here and so are her problems."

"That's not selfish, in fact, I believe it's actually pretty normal."

"I'm trying not to get frustrated about it. I guess I should just suck it up and do my Christian duty for someone who really needs friends right now, but I am struggling with it."

"If she begins to truly upset you and make you uncomfortable, let me know. She can also stay over at my house. It's a little strange having someone you don't know living with you, even temporarily, but we can all adjust. It's Christmas, time for a little miracle."

"Well, let's hope that miracle involves Rufus taking care of the shifter so we can have a little normalcy in our life."

Emma burst out laughing, she couldn't help herself and it was so loud that she woke Brian, who let loose an admirable wail of discontent.

Trying to contain her mirth, Emma bent down to pick him up and, as she softly rocked him back and forth, she swallowed back her tears of laughter.

"What is so damn funny?" Doris asked.

"The thought of Scott and I have ever having a normal life," Emma replied, as she started giggling once again.

CHAPTER 5

The rest of that day passed quietly, which Emma, in particular, was grateful for. She spent most of her time holding Brian and sometimes just staring down at him in his cradle.

It was still hard to believe that he was finally here and now a part of their life.

Her phone started buzzing and she ran over to grab it. Brian was deeply asleep, but she didn't want to take any chance of it waking him up.

"Hi, Shelly," she said quietly.

"Hi, Mom, how are you?"

Emma had called all of her children from the hospital to let them know their little brother had arrived. The boys were pretty excited about it, but Shelly acted as if it had nothing to do with her and, even now, refused to acknowledge him.

"I'm doing well, so is Brian," Emma said, deliberately baiting her daughter to see what the response would be.

"Oh," Shelly was a little surprised by the comment, but refused to respond to it. "Well, anyway, I just wanted to double-check about when you want me to bring over the boys."

"Your father wanted to leave next Saturday, so any time before that would work."

"Yeah, he plans on the three of us doing Christmas with him and Lori next Thursday. I'll probably spend the night there and we can head out on Friday, if that's okay with you."

"That's fine," Emma said, trying not to let her voice reflect her disappointment. She'd hoped they would be coming a little sooner than that, but understood how important it was that they spend time with their father, as well.

"You are going to stay here with us until after Christmas, aren't you?"

Shelly hesitated before responding and Emma's heart froze in her chest for a few seconds.

"Yeah, I will. Liz and Ashley already headed home and they won't be back until the January classes start."

"You can come now if you want."

"Thanks, but I have one more final to take and it's kind of nice to have the place to myself so I can study in peace."

"Alright, well, good luck with it. Have you heard anything more about Madison lately?"

After another hesitation from her end of the line, Shelly replied, "I called her mom because I thought I might try and stop by after my finals, but she was pretty brusque. I don't think Madison has much longer to live and her mom doesn't want us anywhere near her."

Shelly's voice broke and Emma ached to wrap her arms around her daughter and try to comfort her. Madison had also been one of Shelly's college roommates but, over the past summer they had foolishly conducted a séance.

While doing so, a ghost had attached itself to Madison, causing her irreversible physical damage, and Shelly still hadn't quite come to terms with that, which was not unexpected.

However, Shelly had a stubborn streak that wouldn't allow her to let anyone help her work through it, leaving Emma frustrated and worried.

"You know that I'm always here for you if you want talk about any of that." Emma offered yet again.

"I know, but I wouldn't want to pull you away from your time with your new baby."

Emma bit her lip and let that jibe pass with no response. She was used to Shelly shutting her out as far as that subject was concerned, but using Brian as a weapon against her was new, and hurtful.

"Good luck on your final and you drive carefully when you go pick up your brothers, alright?"

"I will, see you soon."

Emma disconnected the call and set the phone down on the end table.

Blowing out a deep breath, she stared down at it, wondering how she was going to deal with this current rift between her and Shelly.

Emma thought they'd gotten past some of their issues over the summer, but there was obviously much more work to be done.

"One step forward, two steps back," Emma murmured. She was fairly confident that once Shelly was here and spent time with the baby, her attitude about him would improve, or so she hoped.

"What's wrong?" Scott asked. He walked up behind her, gently moved her hair to the side and nuzzled her neck as he slid his arms around her.

Emma raised her hand and ran her fingers over his bearded cheek, leaning her head back against his chest, she sighed.

"It's Shelly, she is still having issues about the baby."

"What kind of issues?"

"If I didn't know better, I'd say she's jealous."

"What do we do about that?"

"I have to be sure that I don't ignore her when they come to stay. I'm pretty sure that Brian will win her over all by himself, but it might take some time."

Scott let her out of his grasp and took her hand, leading her over to the cradle so they could gaze down at their sleeping son.

"When are they coming?" Scott asked.

"Not until next Friday. Jeremy is having his Christmas with them Thursday night and they'll head out the following morning."

Scott could hear the sadness in her voice and tried to hold back his anger. Emma so wanted their first Christmas together to be special, to be perfect, and she wanted them to be able to spend as much time together as possible.

She hadn't seen nearly enough of her children over the last year or two and it weighed on her heavily.

"They are still are going to be here for several weeks. You'll have plenty of time with them, Emma, don't let any of this spoil your happiness, not Jeremy and not Shelly."

"I love you," she said, snuggling closer against his side.

"And I love you. You are a fantastic mother, Emma, and your kids know that."

She didn't answer but felt tears welling up in her eyes. Since her divorce, the hardest thing for her to deal with was being separated from her children and, although Scott made her happier than she had ever imagined possible, he couldn't fill that particular hole in her heart.

"Come, sit with me." He still had Emma's hand in his and led her over to the overstuffed glider near the window and sat down, pulling her onto his lap as the chair began to gently move forward and back.

Emma snuggled against him, staring out at the stark winter scenery on the other side of the glass, and let out a long sigh.

"One thing that we've never talked about for some reason," Scott said, "is your parents. Someone taught you well and I'd like to hear about them."

Emma smiled at the memory of her parents as she looked up into Scott's dark brown eyes.

"Where do I start?" she asked, more to herself than to him. "I came into their life when they were in their mid-forties. They had never been able to have a child before then and I was spoiled rotten. I knew that and took advantage of it, well, sometimes I did, not always."

Her voice grew wistful as she thought about her childhood. "I was very close to my dad, he would do anything for me and we had the best times together. My mom was a little more proper and I didn't always fit the mold that she thought I should."

Scott didn't interrupt, he just ran his fingers through Emma's hair and let her continue on at her own pace.

"I didn't know it at the time but, my father had been diagnosed with cancer the summer before I went off to college. I came home for Christmas and noticed he didn't look well, but he and my mom assured me that it was nothing. They chose to keep the truth from me."

She blinked back tears, but her voice was harder when she continued. "He died the following spring, just before I came home for the summer. My mom said he insisted that they hide it from me, so I wouldn't worry."

Emma wiped away the tears that were sliding down her cheeks. Scott tightened his grip on her but said nothing.

"I was so angry at my mother. She took away those few extra months that I could have spent with my dad. I could have helped make them easier for him, but she didn't give me a chance."

Emma's voice trailed off and, although her eyes were still trained on the scenery outside, in her mind was the cold, painful image of her father lying in his casket.

"They were just thinking of you." Scott finally broke his silence.

"You might be right but, at the time, I knew my mother sometimes got jealous of my relationship with my father. In my mind, and in my heart, I blamed her because I thought she wanted him to herself for those last few months."

"And now?"

She shrugged her shoulders. "I really don't know."

"Did you ever mend your relationship with her?"

"Somewhat, we were civil to each other but, we were never close after that. She died of a heart attack when Shelly was just a baby."

"I'm sorry for how that all ended, but it sounds like most of your childhood was happy."

"It was and I try to put the anger and the frustration out of my mind. Although, to be honest I did wallow in it longer than I should have. I think I ended up with Jeremy because of all that happened."

"How so?"

"Jeremy was older than I was. I met him the next year when I went back to college and he was a very take-charge kind of guy even then. My dad had always been there for me and now he wasn't, so I think that I substituted Jeremy for my dad and relied on him to take care of me, to be there for me.

And until a couple of years ago, that's exactly what he did. He made me feel safe, like you do. Unfortunately, I never tried to take care of myself the way I think that I should have, the way I do now."

Scott leaned his head back and raised an eyebrow at her.

"I don't like the way you said that."

"What do you mean?" Emma asked, turning so that she could look into his eyes.

"You make it sound like you jumped from your dad to Jeremy, and when you split with Jeremy, then to me."

"No," she said softly, unable to keep from running her fingers along his bearded jawline and then around his lips.

"I know we've been over this, but maybe now you can understand it better. The reason that I took so long coming back to you was specifically because of what I'd done in the past. I needed to be sure that I was able to take of myself and that I wasn't running into your arms so that you could take care of me.

You don't just fill a void that was left empty by Jeremy, don't ever think that, Scott. I came back to you because you are my soulmate, you are the one person in the world that makes me believe in myself and know that I can do whatever I have to. And you are able to instill confidence in me, while at the same time making sure that I know you'll always be there if I do need you. You make me the best that I can be, and I love you more than I can ever express in just words."

He lowered his head and kissed her full lips, feeling his heart expand and realizing once again how fortunate he was to have her in his life.

Tim arrived the next morning as Emma and Scott were relaxing with a cup of coffee and looked around the kitchen, smelling the lingering odors of eggs and bacon.

Emma saw the expression on his face, and asked, "Would you like some breakfast?"

"I don't want to be any trouble," he replied half-heartedly, and Emma laughed.

"I heard Annie moving around upstairs and was about ready to start cooking for her, anyway."

"As long as it's not a bother, it would really hit the spot."

"What's the matter? Mom on strike? And I thought you were staying here, anyway."

"I had to run home last night, she and I hung out for awhile and I fell asleep on the couch. I will stay here the next few nights though, if you don't mind."

"Of course not," Emma replied, as she tossed strips of bacon into the frying pan.

"I'll leave you guys to it, then," Scott said. "I still have one more snowmobile to get working. Stop out in the barn later, Tim. I'll put you to work."

"Yeah, I'll rush right out," he commented dryly, as Scott pulled on his coat and boots and headed out the back door.

Annie came down a few minutes later and Emma couldn't help but notice how her face brightened when she saw Tim sitting in the kitchen.

"Good morning," Annie said with a smile. There was a spring to her step as she crossed the room and sat down next to him.

"Hello," Tim replied, his smile almost as wide.

Even from across the room, Emma could feel the undercurrent of emotion between them. She was a little surprised, because they hadn't really even had time to get to know one another yet.

"Here you go," she said a few minutes later, setting a plate of bacon and eggs down in front of each of them. "There's coffee on the counter if you want it. I'm going to leave you to your own devices. I have some things to take care of before Brian wakes up."

Annie and Tim picked at their breakfast and talked very little, at least initially. Tim was the more social between he and his brother and he wasn't used to being so tongue-tied around a woman, finding it more than just a little frustrating. He felt like a freaking teenager around her.

"No word from your friend about Jason?" Annie finally asked.

"Not yet, I should probably give him a call later."

"Are you sure it's okay if I keep staying here?"

"Of course, why? Is my brother giving you trouble?"

"Not at all, I was just wondering. I feel like a burden."

"There's no need for that. I imagine you must be getting a little bored though, aren't you?"

"A little," she replied, using her fork to move her food around her plate, eating very little of it. "I try to read or play solitaire, but I feel kind of useless."

Tim's lips were pursed as he watched Annie, and he wished he could help her feel a little less like an unwanted responsibility. In the meantime, he thought it might be in all of their best interests if he got her away from the house for awhile.

"Would you like to go somewhere, do something today?"

Her golden-brown eyes glittered with excitement. "I'd like that, can we go now?"

Tim felt his heart start pounding rapidly in his chest as he stood up, he was excited about being able to spend some time alone with her. But then he stopped and looked around the kitchen.

"Emma went to all the trouble of making us breakfast, let's clean it up and then we'll head out and see what we can find to do."

Annie frowned as she looked around, apparently not thrilled about having to do chores, but Tim grabbed the dishes and headed over to the sink, so she had no choice but to pitch in and help.

It wasn't long before they were done, and Tim stopped out to the barn while Annie ran upstairs to get her coat.

"I'm going to take Annie out for awhile, so I'm not going to be able to help you today. You got it covered?"

Scott stood up from the open engine of one of his newly acquired snowmobiles, wrench in hand and a spot of grease on the end of his nose. He narrowed his eyes at his brother.

"Where are you going?"

Tim shrugged his shoulders. "I'm not sure, she's bored just sitting around so I thought I'd take her out to do something."

"Be careful, we don't know where the shifter is or what he looks like right now."

"You think I don't know that?" Tim asked with a frown.

"I'm just asking you to be careful, don't try to read anything more into it."

"What is your issue with her?"

"Why do you think I have one? Where is that coming from?"

"You make it very obvious, Scott."

"How so?"

"You can barely stand to be in the same room with her. When you are, you interrogate her or just stare at her relentlessly, like you do all of the creatures that we hunt."

"That's not really fair, Tim. I think you are blowing everything out of proportion. She's living in my house and if I have certain reservations about her, that's my business and I'm going to act on them in any way that I see fit.

As of right now, I've been nothing but polite to her, so stop trying to make her out to be some sort of a martyr."

Scott turned back towards the snowmobile engine, putting an end to the conversation. "Have fun and be careful."

Tim's jaw was clenched, and he bit back any further response as he strode angrily out of the barn.

For the first half an hour or so, Tim and Annie just drove around, not talking much but sitting in a comfortable silence. He kept going over his conversation with Scott and wasn't sure how he would ever be able to convince his brother that Annie was the victim, not the target of their suspicions.

Tim did reluctantly acknowledge that Scott wasn't being completely out of line as far as Annie was concerned. He didn't speak to her rudely or make implications about her.

It was more of a vibe that Scott was putting out as far as she was concerned, and Tim wondered if it was something that only he was picking up on.

He and Scott spent most of their adult life hunting together, and there were many times when they had to rely on non-verbal cues from one another. Their ability to do so had saved their lives more times than he could count. And maybe that was what he was getting from Scott now, and simply hadn't realized it.

"Hey, did you see that sign?" Tim asked suddenly, pulling his thoughts back to the present and turning in Annie's direction.

"No, what did it say?"

"There's a craft show every weekend until Christmas. That town is just five miles away, want to go check it out?"

It was certainly nothing that he would ever have considered for himself, but he thought she might enjoy it.

"Sure," Annie replied, just happy to be out of the house and in his company. She wasn't as comfortable around Scott or Emma, and really enjoyed being able to sit back and relax.

They arrived in the busy little township a few minutes later and began to wander through the various booths, stopping for hot cocoa, checking out the gifts for sale, some beautifully handcrafted, others cheap and gaudy.

"Do you want to get something for your grandmother?" Tim asked.

"My what? Oh, no, that's okay. I talked to her this morning and we're going to celebrate the holidays sometime after the new year. I thought that was far enough out in the future that I wouldn't be lying to her. I wasn't, was I?"

"What do you mean?"

They stopped walking and she turned towards him, her hazel eyes were wide and her lips were pursed in frustration. Tim could just barely see a vein throbbing wildly in her neck above the colorful scarf she was wearing.

"I'll be able to live my own life again soon, right? This can't go on indefinitely."

"I know," Tim said, releasing a long, deep breath. "It must be hard for you, but we really are only concerned about your safety, and we will do everything we can to get your life back to normal, as soon as we can."

"Are you spending time with me today just to make sure that I don't bolt?"

The cold breeze made her cheeks flush a pretty pink color and her dark brown curls were swirling in an attractive cloud around her face.

Tim wanted to reach out and bury his fingers in her hair and pull her up close against his body but, instead he let out a long breath, trying to get his body back under control.

He brushed his fingers over her porcelain cheek, then around her lips, feeling his pulse quicken when they parted in response, as if waiting to be kissed.

"Not at all," he replied, his voice a little huskier than normal, "and please don't feel like you are a prisoner. You can leave anytime that you want. I just hope that you'll talk to me before you decide to do that. I don't want you to get hurt."

She looked up into his soft brown eyes and Annie could see that he really was concerned about her, she just questioned why, because they barely knew each other.

"Why does this matter so much to you? I don't think Emma or Scott would blink an eye if I said I was leaving, but you, you seem to be making this personal."

Tim smiled and allowed himself to reach out and take her hands in his. "It is personal to me. There is something about you that tugs at my heartstrings. I worry about you and want to keep you safe."

He lowered his eyes, embarrassed by his own words. "I feel like you need us, and I want to be there for you. I hope that doesn't make you uncomfortable."

Cautiously, he raised his eyes to hers, not sure what her reaction would be to his spontaneous, and surprisingly intimate, comments.

Tim was relieved to see a soft smile on her lips as she returned his gaze.

"It doesn't make me uncomfortable," she replied. "Just the opposite, actually. The more time that I spend with you, the safer and more comfortable I feel. Thank you for looking after me."

Annie stepped closer and stood on her tiptoes as she kissed his cheek. Keeping a tight hold on one of his hands, she turned and made her way down the alley through the various tents. There was a bounce in her step and her heart felt lighter than it had in some time.

CHAPTER 6

Scott had continued to seethe silently after Tim left, and eventually found himself so distracted that he couldn't concentrate any further and made his way back to the house.

He finally located Emma, who was rocking Brian in the nursery and, when he took in that sight, Scott felt himself immediately beginning to calm down.

He pulled over another chair so he could get a closer look at his sleeping son.

"What's wrong, Scott?"

He let loose a long, frustrated breath and met her brilliant green eyes. "I don't feel one hundred percent confident about Annie, and Tim and I are really butting heads about her. It's maddening."

"What do you think is the problem with her?"

He considered Emma's question and, once he'd straightened out his thoughts, he tried to find a way to explain what he was feeling.

"I always trust my instincts and they are on red alert about her for some reason. But, because Tim thinks so highly of her, I keep doubting my own reactions. I'm on a freaking roller-coaster as far as she's concerned, and I don't know what to think about her from one minute to the next."

"Are you worried that she could be a shifter?"

"That is a possibility."

"Any other possible options?"

"Well, even if she isn't a shifter, she could have an emotional tie to the creature that's making her seem off."

"Wouldn't you expect that she would have an emotional tie to Jason. I mean, he was her boyfriend, so even if she didn't know what he was, she did care for him."

"True, and that's the premise we are going on; she didn't know what he was and is now afraid of him. But, what if that isn't the case, at all? What if she did know what he was?"

"I don't understand," Emma said. The baby's sleep was restless and she wondered if it was because of their conversation.

"Let me put him in the cradle. Meet me in our sitting room and we can finish this."

A few minutes later, she was snuggled up alongside Scott on the loveseat.

"Alright," Emma said, tucking her feet up underneath her body as she tried to get comfortable, "what did you mean about her knowing what he was?"

"I think most normal humans would react pretty strongly if they found out their love interest was a monster, but what if he has some kind of hold over her?"

"I don't follow you."

"I'm just speculating, but have you ever heard of Stockholm syndrome?"

"No, what is that?"

"It's a condition where someone, usually in a hostage situation, develops a psychological alliance with their captor. I'm only throwing it out as a possibility. Maybe she didn't know in the beginning, but has since succumbed to this disorder and feels some sort of a loyalty to the creature. Shifter syndrome, so to speak."

Emma rolled her eyes at his attempted humor, then said, "One, she could be a shifter or two, she could be a shifter sympathizer. If Annie is neither of those things, what's left?"

Scott wrapped his arm around Emma and pulled her up close against his side. He lightly kissed the top of her head as he considered that question.

"Unfortunately, what's left might be the worst possibility of all, for Tim, anyway."

"What do you mean?"

"We've both noticed that she isn't normal, do we agree on that?"

"I'm not sure I'd put it that way, but there is definitely something different about her."

"Well, it could be that she is just a damaged young woman. And if that's the issue, Tim might be taking on more than he realizes."

"If this was a case you were working on, what would you do now?"

"Rule out what isn't the truth and narrow down the options until I know what is."

"For both of our peace of mind, and so that your relationship with Tim isn't damaged irreparably, you need to do that. Now, tell me how you plan on accomplishing it."

"You're kind of bossy, aren't you?"

Emma smiled up into his deep brown eyes and lost herself in them momentarily. Scott cupped her head with his hand and gently pulled her towards him, kissing her long and thoroughly.

"Don't change the subject," she whispered breathlessly.

"Let me think. If this was a real case, the first thing I'd do would be go to her hometown and double-check who she really is. Confirm her employment, where she lives, talk to some neighbors, things like that."

"So, do it."

"What, now?"

"Why not, she just lives a couple of hours away. It'll be the first step in our ruling out any specific problems as far as she is concerned."

"But, don't you need me here to help out with Brian?"

"I'll be fine for the afternoon," Emma replied, biting back a smile. "Get dressed and do your best Fed impersonation, but you cannot shave off the beard, not yet."

"Deal," he replied, and hurried off to change his persona and head off to begin his investigation, happy that he was finally able to do something productive about the doubts that were eating away at him.

Scott stopped by Annie's apartment building a couple of hours later and the first thing he noticed was the large sign bolted to the brick wall outside the main doors which read: No Pets Allowed.

Finding the entrance doors unlocked, Scott made his way inside and located her apartment number on the second floor. It was a fairly small building with only about twelve apartments between the two floors.

It was the middle of a workday and very quiet. Annie's apartment was about halfway down the hall. Scott knocked on a few doors down one direction from her apartment but got no response. Heading down the other way, he heard a TV playing loudly behind one door and, feeling encouraged, he vigorously knocked on it.

A woman, who appeared to be somewhere in her late sixties, opened the door slightly, leaving the security chain latched as she peered suspiciously out at Scott.

"Excuse me, Ma'am," he said, lifting his fake badge up so she could see it clearly. "I'm looking for some information on one of your neighbors, would you be able to help me?"

Her plump face lit up conspiratorially and she hurriedly closed the door, unlatched the chain, and then quickly re-opened it to allow him in.

"Which neighbor?" she asked excitedly.

"First, may I ask you name?"

"Of course, Mary Armstrong. Are you FBI?"

"That's what the badge says, Ms. Armstrong."

"Please, call me Mary. This is so exciting. I've been here over ten years, who do you want to know about? Can I get you tea?"

She was wearing a yellow housedress covered with colorful flowers that made Scott's head hurt if he looked at it too closely.

Mary led him into her living room, which was approximately four steps from the door, and offered him a seat on one of her large, overstuffed chairs.

"Thank you. I'm looking for information on Annie Kincaid, her apartment is just the down the hall from yours."

"Oh, yes," Mary said softly, nodding her head as if she knew this day would come eventually. "What did she do?"

"Nothing," he replied, "someone reported her missing. She's apparently been gone for a few days."

"That's true, she hasn't been home since early this week."

Playing his role, Scott asked, "Do you have any idea where she might have gone?"

"No, she never has visitors. I don't think she even has any friends, although she usually goes out most nights. I don't know where she goes but, usually, she doesn't come back until very late, after I'm asleep."

"She never has guests?"

"None that I'm aware of."

"Do you know her very well?"

"No, I've tried talking to her. I even took her over a bundt cake when she first moved in, but she's very standoffish."

"How long has she lived here?"

"About six months," Mary said, and Scott was surprised at that because it was also the exact length of time that Annie had been with Jason.

"Have you noticed anything unusual about her?"

"Like what?"

"Anything at all that struck you as a little odd."

"Not really, other than the dog incident."

"What happened?"

"My good friend, Chloe Robichar, has a little yorkie, Sparky. She always brings the dog with her when she comes to visit and he wouldn't hurt a flea, but Annie pitched a fit when she ran into Chloe and Sparky in the hallway.

She started screaming at her to get the dog out of the building, that she would report her, all kinds of vile things came out of her mouth. It was shocking."

"Was the dog doing anything to her?"

"It was barking its fool head off and causing quite a fuss, but it weighs about five pounds and certainly wasn't going to hurt Annie. She did report me to management so Chloe can't bring him here anymore," Mary added bitterly.

Scott handed her his card, then said, "Please call me if she shows up, or if you think of anything else that might help us find her. I do appreciate your help."

He couldn't locate anyone else in the apartment building that knew Annie, so he headed over to the dentist's office where Annie worked.

There was a young woman, probably mid-twenties, sitting behind the glass divider when Scott walked into the waiting room.

She slid the glass back and smiled prettily at him as he approached. He held out his badge for a brief moment, then stuck it back into his jacket pocket. The smile dropped from her face at the sight of the badge and her brown eyes widened.

"Can I help you?" she asked, and Scott took a moment to look around the waiting room, relieved to see that it was empty.

"Yes, Ma'am, I'm looking for some information. Can I have your name, please?"

"Kelli Jensen." There was a tremor in her voice now and she was beginning to look frightened. Or maybe guilty, Scott realized, wondering what she'd done that would make her so uncomfortable around law enforcement.

"I'm looking for information on Annie Kincaid, does she work here?"

The girl's face relaxed a little when she realized that he was not here for her. She let out a long, relieved breath and nodded her head.

"Well, yes and no," she said, qualifying her answer. "She isn't here today. In fact, she's been gone for a few days and we don't know when she'll be back."

"Where did she go?"

Kelli shrugged her shoulders and looked around behind her, she wanted to make sure no other employees were within earshot.

She leaned forward and, lowering her voice substantially, Kelli said, "Some sort of emergency came up and Annie called in. She didn't have any idea when she might be back. Is she in trouble?"

Scott rested his arm on the ledge that extended out into the waiting room and met her eyes. "We're just trying to get a little background information on her, that's all. You're about the same age as she is, aren't you? Were you two friends?"

"Oh, she is actually a few years older than I am." Kelli sounded a bit insulted by his comment and started biting her lip.

"You aren't friends with her?"

She gnawed on her lip a moment more with her perfectly whitened teeth and then finally let it loose so she could respond. "No, she was always pretty stand-offish, not a very friendly person. We spoke causally here at work but that's all."

"You never talked about her life outside of work? About her relationships?"

"No, not ever."

"Is there anyone else here who might know about her personal life?"

"No, I don't think so. There are a few other women that work here and I am friends with them. We've all discussed this very issue together."

"What issue?"

"How unfriendly and closed off Annie is."

"Are they here now?"

Kelli looked around once again, then down at the little clock situated on her side of the glass wall. "No, they all went to lunch and aren't back yet. Dr. McMackin, the dentist, isn't here either. I'm all by myself."

"How long have you known Annie?"

Kelli's brow furrowed as she thought about that. "She started here in the summer, June, I think."

"About six months ago?" Scott asked.

Kelli nodded her head and gave Scott a speculative look. She was dying of curiosity about why he was so interested in Annie Kincaid, but he had no intention of satisfying that curiosity.

"Thanks for all your help, Miss Jensen. You keep out of trouble, understand?"

Her cheeks flushed prettily, and she lowered her eyes, wondering if he maybe knew more about her than he was letting on. Scott let her wonder and made his way back out into the parking lot.

Starting the engine of his car, he sat quietly for a few moments while it warmed up. Annie must have come to town just six months ago, that's when she got her apartment and that's when she got her job. It's also when she met and started dating Jason.

Scott began to get very curious about Annie's life before that time and thought maybe he'd see if Rufus could look into it. But he had to work surreptitiously, behind his brother's back, and he didn't like the feel of that, so he decided to think about it for a bit before taking that particular step.

"What did you find out?" Emma asked, a few hours later when he returned home.

"Where are Tim and Annie?"

"They were gone most of the day and went straight upstairs when they got back."

He took Emma's hand and led her over into their private sitting room, where he could be sure they wouldn't be overheard.

"The only unusual information that I got was that she not only moved into that apartment six months ago, but that's also when she started working at the dentist's office."

"Isn't that how long she'd been dating Jason?"

Their eyes met and Scott nodded. "Yes, it's strange, isn't it? She would have had to meet him almost the day she arrived and immediately start up a relationship."

"Is that so unusual? She's an attractive woman."

"I guess not, it's just all these little things that are slightly off-kilter keep popping up. They aren't glaringly obvious issues, but they are really triggering my spidey senses."

"What now?"

"I'm thinking about asking Rufus to look into her past, but I don't want him to go running to Tim about it, so I'm going to hold off on that, for now, anyway."

"So, what next?"

"I'm going to head over to my mother's tomorrow and check out some of the books we have there. Next step is to rule her out as a shifter and I'm not quite sure how. I'll do a little research, maybe even check in with Nathan about it. How are you doing anyway?"

"Getting better every day," she replied, rising on her tiptoes so she could wrap her arms around his neck and caress his lips with her own.

CHAPTER 7

"Morning, Mom," Scott called out the next day, as he stepped through her front door and took off his boots and coat.

Doris hurried in from the kitchen with Tolstoy right behind her. The dog ran over to Scott and, once he realized who it was, his tail started wagging spastically until Scott couldn't hold off any longer and rough-housed with him for a couple of minutes before his mom yelled at both of them.

"Stop it before you break something."

With one last ruffle of the dog's fur, Scott turned towards Doris. "Smells like fresh-brewed coffee in here. You wouldn't have any extra, would you?"

"Of course, I would. Sit down and make yourself comfortable. What are you doing here, anyway, shouldn't you be home helping Emma?"

Doris set a full cup down in front of him and couldn't miss the lines of tension across his forehead. He obviously had something on his mind.

"Can you talk about it?"

Scott lifted his eyes to hers, hesitated for just a moment and then nodded. "First, I have to ask if you can keep what I'm going to say to yourself."

"Of course, I can," she replied, slightly offended.

"From Tim?"

"Why? What's going on?" Doris asked, sitting down across the table from him.

"It's that girl, Annie. Every instinct in my body is screaming out that there is something wrong with her, but when I try to talk to Tim about it, he gets angry and he will not listen."

"He has feelings for her?"

"Looks like it and they are getting stronger every day, or maybe I'm just pushing him that way."

"What are your concerns?"

"We don't even know for sure that she isn't a shifter, that's why I'm here. I need to check out some of the lore and find out how I can vet her. The only way that I know involves a knife and a deep incision and I don't see either Tim or Annie being agreeable to that, so I have to find some other way."

"What can I do?" she asked, her brows drawing together in concern.

"We'll talk more after I do some research. If you could keep this between us for now, I would appreciate that."

"Certainly."

Scott poured through various tomes for the next hour or two but was unable to find that answers that he needed. He leaned back in the heavy leather chair and ran his fingers roughly through his hair.

With a heavy sigh, he picked up his phone and called Nathan Michaels.

"What's up, Scott?"

"Merry Christmas, Nathan. How are you and Polly doing?"

"She's baking away like a fiend and I'm hiding in my lab. How about you? Congratulations on the baby, by the way. I heard you named after your dad, I'm sure that would make him very proud."

"Thanks, Nathan, word has certainly spread fast, hasn't it?"

"It's a small and very tight-knit community that we have, Scott. Like it or not."

"Too true."

"What can I do for you?"

"I need some information, if you have a minute."

"For you, of course, I do."

"I know that I can vet a shifter with a knife and deep cut to one of their vital organs but, if that isn't an option, is there any other way to rule out if someone is a shifter?"

"Is this for the same case that Tim and Rufus are working on?"

"Part of it, yeah."

"Hold on a second, let me grab my research." Scott waited patiently on the phone while Nathan rustled through his piles of papers.

"Here we are," Nathan said a few moments later. "Silver will burn them, from what I understand. I don't know why, maybe something they carry in their blood, but they can't even touch it without showing some indication of discomfort."

"You mean, like silverware?"

"Perfect utensil to use, they'd never suspect what you were trying to do. You are trying to rule someone out, aren't you?"

Scott once again appreciated how astute Nathan could be and what a great ally he was in their constant battles against the dark entities of the world.

"Yes, I am, and I think I can find a way to do that."

"I'm in the process of putting together information on shifters," Nathan said. "We rarely come across them so accurate data is limited. I would appreciate hearing any details you have after you've tried this approach. I'll add it to my dossier."

"I'll definitely keep you posted. Thanks, again, Nathan. I knew you'd have the answer that I needed. Wish Polly a Merry Christmas for me and take care."

"You, too, and please call if there is anything else that I can do."

Scott sat quietly contemplating what Nathan had told him and then picked up his phone and called Emma.

"Seriously, those cheap bastards gave us stainless steel silverware for the wedding? Not actual silver?"

"That's correct, but I'm not sure I'd call your friends cheap bastards just because they didn't want to empty their bank accounts for us. Why are you asking?"

"Shifters apparently get burnt if they touch silver. Now, I just have to find some and put it in Annie's way so I can rule that out once and for all."

"How are you going to do that?"

"Looks like I'll have to enlist my mother's aid. I'm almost positive she has real silver."

"You won't be putting her in any danger, will you?"

"Of course not. No worries, I'll see you in a bit."

He found his mother curled up on the couch reading a book and sat down beside her.

"I have to ask a favor of you."

"What?" she asked, eying him suspiciously.

"Your silverware is actual silver, isn't it?"

"The good ones are, yes. Why do you ask?"

"According to Nathan, real silver will burn a shifter. He said there is no way they can hide their discomfort if they come in contact with it. I thought maybe you'd want to invite Tim and Annie over for dinner tomorrow."

"You are so devious, Scott. You must have gotten that from your father."

He winked at her, and said, "I don't think there would be any danger to you, whatsoever, but if you feel uncomfortable about it, or about being deceitful to Tim, you don't have to do this."

Doris placed a bookmark in the book and set it down on the end table as she thought over his request.

"If she has no problems with the silverware, that will answer your questions once and for all, right? Then we can relax and not worry so much about having her around?"

"It will completely rule her out as a shifter."

"What do I do if she has a reaction?"

"Absolutely nothing. You'll be able to see any physical reaction and you'll know, but don't let on. If she is a shifter then she is also a very accomplished liar. She'll come up with some sort an excuse so that she doesn't have to touch the silverware after that."

"And I just pretend that I didn't notice?"

"Exactly, you can give me a call after they leave and let me know what happened. If she is a shifter, I'll take it up with Tim, you don't have to get involved with that part of it."

"But he will know that I was complicit in this little scheme, and he will be very angry at both of us."

"If she's a shifter, he'll get over it. He would never, knowingly, put our family at risk and he'll realize this was necessary."

Doris sat quietly for a few moments, weighing her guilt at deceiving her son versus the potential danger that Annie could present. She realized there was no need for any further debate on the issue.

"I'll call Tim in a little while and invite them over. I've been toying with the idea of whether or not I should put up my fake

Christmas tree, so maybe we can do that. I'll use it as my excuse to get them over here."

"You're just a bit devious yourself, Mother," he replied. "Thanks for doing this."

Giving her a kiss on the cheek, Scott got ready to head back home, feeling almost light-hearted that this issue should be resolved soon, which would finally allow him to relax and enjoy the holidays with his new family.

"Welcome," Doris said, as she opened the door and allowed Annie and Tim in. Tolstoy came running in from the kitchen to greet his guests but slid to a stop in front of the two of them.

He was still a pup but was already good-sized and looked quite intimidating when he got protective. The hair on the back of his neck rose and he started barking, a loud, sharp bark that was coming from deep down in his chest.

They all looked at him in confusion and Tim tried to reach out to let Tolstoy sniff his hand, thinking he didn't recognize him with his heavy winter coat on, but the dog backed away in fear and continued to bark.

Doris had a concerned look on her face when she snapped her fingers in front of his face to get his attention. He stopped barking but kept turning his head to stare at Tim and Annie.

Annie had slid behind Tim, using him as a buffer between her and Tolstoy.

"You didn't tell me she had a dog," Annie said, somewhat accusingly.

"Sorry, it didn't cross my mind. What's up with him, Mom?"

"I don't know, let me go put him in his crate. I can't have him behaving like this around guests. Apparently, it's something I'll have to work on with him."

Doris grabbed his collar and led him upstairs to her bedroom where she kept his crate. By the time she returned to the living room, Annie and Tim had removed their coats and boots and were making themselves comfortable.

"Thanks for coming over to help me. I was going back and forth with the idea of decorating the tree, so it's a little late going up this year. Will you run into the basement and bring up the tree, Tim? I already brought up most of the containers with the decorations, but that's a little bulky and I have trouble maneuvering it on the stairs."

"Sure," Tim replied, heading down to get it.

"Annie, I fixed a pot roast for dinner, I hope that's something you enjoy."

"Yes, I love it," she replied.

"Tell me about yourself, where do you normally spend Christmas?"

Annie raised her hazel eyes to meet Doris' and didn't answer immediately.

Shrugging her shoulders, she finally replied, "Sometimes, I spend it with my Grandmother, other times, all by myself."

"No one should spend Christmas alone," Doris said, feeling a little sad for the young lady.

"I don't mind being alone." Annie replied, there was no emotion in the statement, she was just stating a fact.

"Well, regardless, I'm glad you can be with us this year. Tell me about yourself."

Annie looked at her as if she'd just asked her to recite the Declaration of Independence. "Why?"

"My son seems to care a great deal for you, and I care for him. I thought it would be nice if you and I got to know each other a little better."

"Is that why you invited us over tonight?"

"Yes, I do need help with that damn tree, but I thought we could share a meal and decorate it together. Sharing time together is what the holidays are all about, after all."

"I see."

Damn, Doris said to herself, *this one's a tough nut to crack.*

She was saved from trying to make any further small-talk when they heard the groaning, bumping and banging as Tim finally made his way up the narrow staircase with the heavy, artificial tree. With an expression of pure relief, he tossed the bagged tree over into the corner where it was usually displayed.

"Thanks, Tim, you didn't break anything in the process, did you?"

"Not as far as I know," he replied with a smile.

The timer in the kitchen went off and Doris stood up and rubbed her hands together. "My biscuits are done. Tim, do you think you can get that put together, at least some of it, now? I have to put the final touches on dinner and after that we can decorate the tree, if the two of you would like to assist me."

"Sure, Annie and I can get it put together in no time, go do whatever it is you have to in the kitchen."

"Thanks," she replied, and hurried out to save her biscuits from burning.

A short time later, Tim and Annie made their way into the kitchen where Doris was bustling around.

"The roast in on the cutting board on the island. Would you like to do the honors with that, Tim? Annie, the table is all set, please have a seat wherever you'd like."

Doris kept her eye on Annie while she finished dishing up the mashed potatoes, once they were on the table and Tim finished cutting the roast, they'd be ready to sit down and eat.

Annie still hadn't taken a place at the table when Doris set the heavy bowl down in the center of it.

"Please, have a seat. What can I get you to drink?"

"Water is fine," Annie replied, looking down at the elaborate table setting. "It looks very nice."

"Thank you. How about you, Tim, what would you like to drink?"

"Water's good for me, too," he replied, lifting the meat platter and carrying it over towards the table.

The suspense was killing Doris as she waited for Annie to sit down and touch her fork or knife. She truly had no idea what the result would be of their little test, but she wanted it over with. The deception that she was perpetrating on her son was making her more uncomfortable by the minute and she wanted it resolved, one way or the other.

Doris couldn't help looking over towards Annie frequently. The girl was behaving quite oddly, walking around the table with her hand out slightly, hovering over the table settings as she moved around. Her face was blank and Doris had no idea what she could be possibly be thinking.

"Is everything alright, Annie?" Tim asked, he'd noticed her unusual behavior, as well.

"I'm so sorry, Tim. I would really like to sit down and enjoy this lovely meal, but I'm not feeling well."

"What's wrong?" he asked, moving over closer to her.

"It started earlier this afternoon, I've been having sharp pains in my stomach and feel nauseous. It seems to be getting worse."

"Why didn't you say something earlier?"

"I was looking forward to getting to know your mother," she said, with a wan smile in Doris' direction. "And I was sincerely hoping I'd feel better by now, but I don't think I can eat a bite. Doris has gone to so much trouble, you sit down and eat. I think I might go lay down on the couch for a few minutes."

She walked into the living room and Tim and Doris just looked at one another for a moment. Tim stared down at the feast on the table, his mouth watering at the delicious aromas swirling around him, and his stomach growled in rebellion when it realized what he was thinking.

"I'm so sorry, Mom, but I'd better take her home now. Thank you for going to all this trouble for us. Maybe we can come back tomorrow."

"Don't worry about it, Tim. I'm just sorry that Annie isn't feeling well. Let me fix you a doggie bag."

"No, you don't have to do that," he replied, but the response was half-hearted, and Doris knew it.

Tim and Annie left a few minutes later, along with a large plastic bag filled with Rubbermaid containers.

Doris made her way upstairs to let Tolstoy out of his kennel, the dog had continued to bark while he was up there, but with the door closed it was muted and hard to hear.

He rushed past her as soon as the door was opened and ran downstairs, manically smelling everywhere that Annie had been.

Doris' eyes were narrowed as she watched the dog, then she made her way over to the phone to call Scott.

"What's the verdict?" he asked, seeing the caller ID.

"There is none," she replied, sounding a bit defeated.

"What do you mean?"

"She felt sick and they both left before we ate. The table was all set, she walked around it but never sat down and never touched any of the silverware."

"Damn," Scott said, and even though Doris couldn't see him, she knew he was running his fingers through his hair in frustration.

"Do you believe her? Was she really not feeling well?"

"I can't say for sure one way or the other. She seemed fine right up until we were going to sit down, but who knows, it could have been for real. I'm sorry that I couldn't help, son."

"Don't worry, Mom. We'll find another way. Thanks for doing that though."

"You're welcome, and Scott?"

"Yes?"

"Annie really is a strange bird. I don't know if she's actually dangerous or not, but she is unlike anyone that I've ever met before."

"I know, that's what keeps tripping me up with her. Take care, we'll talk soon."

"What's the verdict?" Emma asked, she'd walked in the room about halfway through his conversation with his mother and could tell it had not gone as expected.

Scott shook and head and pursed his lips in frustration. "She was sick and couldn't eat a thing."

Their eyes met and Emma said what they were both thinking.

"That's sounds a little suspicious. Could she have known about the silverware?"

"I don't know, but I'll see what I can find out."

"Tanya?"

"She's probably our best bet, you okay with that?"

Scott had a lengthy relationship with Tanya Merrimac before he got together with Emma. She was a beautiful, strong woman who had helped with the situation they ran into earlier in the year at the annual Hunter's Gathering.

She and Emma had managed to work together, but neither of them planned to ever have anything to do with one another after that situation was resolved.

"Go ahead, call her," Emma said. "Will she even talk to you?"

"I don't know, guess we'll find out."

Emma took a deep breath and swallowed down the jealousy trying to swim to the surface as she pictured the curvaceous, blue-eyed witch that had enchanted Scott for a significant period of time.

"I'll give you some privacy."

"Emma," Scott said, reaching out and grabbing her hand as she walked by. She spun around and he wrapped his arms securely around her and kissed her long and hard.

"It's just a phone call. I don't have to make it to her if you don't want me to."

Emma was almost embarrassed by her insecurity and gently ran her fingers along Scott's scruffy jawline. "I'm not worried, do what you have to do."

He watched her walk out of the room with her shoulders squared and her head held high and couldn't help but smile. How that woman could even imagine that he would have eyes for another was beyond him.

Still he hesitated before calling Tanya, he didn't want to give her the wrong impression, but he really could use her help.

"Scott," Tanya's sultry voice came over the line after just a few short rings, "what a pleasant surprise. Is something wrong?"

"No, thanks for taking my call, Tanya. I hope you're well."

"I am and you?"

"Very good. I could use some help on a case though. Do you have a minute?"

"Sure, what do you need?" He could almost hear her disappointment over the line.

"What can you tell me about silver?"

Tanya wanted to slam the phone down and never hear his baritone voice again, but she couldn't bring herself to do that.

"As far as what?"

"I guess I'm interested in its properties. Does it have any vibrational qualities, or does it exude any type of energy?"

"Silver is a mineral which doesn't generally give off energy. But, having said that, it is considered a stimulator. It can create an energy increase in a person if they wear it."

"But no vibrations or anything like that?"

"Silver is related to the moon and the moon's energies. Pure silver is capable of removing and redistributing negative energy, but I'm not sure about vibrations."

Her soft voice trailed off as she tried to recall what other information she'd learned about silver.

"I believe it is considered the best thermal and electrical conductor of all the metals and it's used a lot for electrical applications. Some metals can carry sound, but I'm not sure if silver is one of them. Does any of this help?"

"Somewhat, yes. Do you think that if someone was attuned to it or if they tended to have some sort of reaction to it, like an allergy, they could be sensitive enough to silver without even touching it?"

"That's a good question, I think it's possible. The extent of their reaction to it would probably be the gauge as far as how easily they would be aware of it."

Scott started talking as he thought over what's she'd said, trying to make sure he understood.

"So, if someone had a severe reaction to silver, they could possibly know what it was without even having to come into direct contact with it?"

"Yes, that's what I think."

"Thank you, Tanya. I appreciate your help and I really do hope that you are doing well."

"You're welcome," she replied. "And Scott?"

"Yes?"

"Please don't ever call me again."

"What do we do now?" Emma asked, later that evening while they were relaxing against the padded headboard of their bed.

"I truly don't know. I am beyond frustrated because every time that a question comes up, or possible solution arrives, we get an unqualified answer. Nothing definite to know for sure what we're dealing with."

"You don't think the info Tanya gave you indicates that Annie may well have been able to feel or get a sense that the silverware was indeed silver?"

"I do think it's possible, very possible," he replied, running his fingers through his hair. "But it's not a definite answer. I still have to find some way to prove it, so we can be sure."

"What if you can't?"

A little half-smile appeared on his face. "I will not give up, Emma. One way or the other I'll confirm what she is, trust me on that."

CHAPTER 8

Emma remained sore and tired for a few days but, with the dawning of each new day, she grew stronger and felt more and more like herself.

The time passed quickly, and it was just a couple of days later that Gabriel and Hannah knocked at their back door one morning, interrupting Emma, who was giving Scott a lesson on the proper way to hold a baby.

"Come on in," Emma said, heading over to give each of them a hug as they stepped into the kitchen. "Can I get you some coffee?"

"Thanks, Emma, that would be great. I guess you decided to go ahead and have the kid before we got back," Gabriel said with a goofy smile, as he took off his boots and hung his coat on the rack next to the door.

Callie got up from her bed in the corner to greet them, she had a real soft spot for Gabriel and her tail wagged incessantly.

He bent down and wrapped his arms around her neck, sinking his fingers into her thick fur. "Good to see you, too, girl," he said, then stood and stepped over towards and Scott and Brian, looking a little unsure of himself.

"Are you both doing well?" Hannah asked, looking curiously at Emma. She was a sweet, young girl, exceptionally shy, but as time went by, she was coming out of her shell more and more.

"We are, thank you. Aren't you two back earlier than you planned?"

"A little," she replied, wrapping a long strand of blonde hair behind her ear as she moved over closer to Scott and the baby. "We heard there was a storm coming so we thought we'd get out ahead of it."

"Would you like to hold him?" Scott asked, and Hannah's face lit up.

"May I?"

"Of course," Scott said, as she sat down next to him and he gently handed the sleeping bundle over to her.

Hannah blushed when his fingers touched hers during the transfer, but Scott pretended that he hadn't noticed.

"What did you name him?" Gabriel asked, wisps of his red hair escaping from the brightly colored tuque still set securely on his head.

"Brian John Devereaux," Scott said, his brown eyes glowing with pride and love. "New hat?"

"Yeah, my mom gave it to me."

"How's she doing?" Emma asked, as she set a cup of coffee down in front of Hannah and then at the empty seat next to her. Gabriel was still standing, peering over Hannah's shoulder at the little cherub in her arms.

"Good, real good. She wishes we lived closer, but she understands. Oh, by the way we have presents."

"Little early, aren't they?"

"Not Christmas presents, baby presents. This is from my mom," he said, grabbing a large decorative bag and handing it to Emma.

"How adorable, look Scott." Emma pulled out a brown fleece jumpsuit with ears on the hood.

"Looks like a bear, or maybe Bigfoot," Scott said, with a lopsided grin in Gabriel's direction.

"Holy crap balls, I don't think she even thought about that, sorry."

"I'm kidding," Scott said, amazed how easy it was to get the kid going, even after all this time.

"Oh, right," he replied, letting out a deep breath.

"I love it, please be sure to give me her address so I can thank her properly, that was very thoughtful."

"Will do, and this one is from us."

Hannah had a strange expression on her face as Emma dug into the gift bag, and Emma couldn't help asking, "Is there something wrong, Hannah?"

"No," she replied with a heavy sigh, "it's just that Gabriel picked it out."

He did have an unusual style and Emma couldn't imagine what she might find in the bag. She gingerly pulled out the onesie and then started giggling.

It was gray with large black wording on the front that said "Storm Pooper" along with a picture of a jedi warrior.

"I love it," she replied, holding it up for Scott to see. "Thank you."

"There were so many to choose from. I really wanted to get the one that said, "It's all shits and giggles until someone giggles and shits" or even "All mommy wanted was a backrub", but Hannah wouldn't let me."

"This one is perfect."

Brian starting fussing right then and Hannah's eyes widened in panic.

"I think he's hungry, so I'll take him now," Emma said, and Hannah quickly handed him over.

Callie had immediately taken the baby into her fold and generally had to be in whatever room Brian was in, so she hurried along after Emma who left to find a little privacy.

"Anything interesting happen while we were gone?"

"As a matter of fact, it did," Scott replied.

Gabriel was aware of Scott and Tim's line of work, but Scott still hesitated to share everything with him. Gabriel never held back the fact that he discussed pretty much everything with Hannah and, although Scott had a certain amount of trust in the girl, he didn't think she, or by extension, Gabriel, needed to know about all the creatures and dangers that existed, usually unseen, in their world.

Hannah was a sweet, innocent, young girl and Scott didn't see the point in unnecessarily burdening her with things that she didn't need to know.

"We have someone staying here," he began, and the two of them looked at him curiously.

"I thought you were going to wait till after the first of the year."

"We are," he replied, "but this is a special case. She was involved in a dangerous situation and we are letting her stay here until we can get that taken care of for her."

"Just one woman, then?" Hannah asked, then looked down into her cup. She had trouble speaking directly to Scott, or Tim, but she still engaged in conversation with them much more than she did when she and Gabriel had first arrived.

"Yes, her name is Annie. She's upstairs right now."

Picking up her spoon and swirling it around her cup, Hannah asked, "Does Emma need me to do any cooking or baking?"

The plan was for Hannah to handle all the kitchen work once they did start taking in B & B guests at the house.

"You can confirm with her, but I don't think so. Annie has been eating with us or in her room. We aren't doing anything special as far as she is concerned."

"If Emma does need me, please just let me know, I'd be happy to help out."

"Thanks, Hannah, we appreciate that. What about this storm that's coming? I haven't been paying attention to the news lately."

"It's not going to be horrible, but they say this area could get six to ten inches over the next couple of days."

"That's actually good news. Emma's boys will be here later this week and maybe we'll have enough snow on the ground that we can take them snowmobiling or cross-country skiing."

"Sweet," Gabriel said, and his eyes lit up at the thought of it.

"You got a few minutes right now?" Scott asked.

"Sure, for what?"

"Let's head out to the barn, we can check the generator and the sleds. We'll make sure everything is ready, just in case we do get slammed by that storm."

Hannah watched the two of them bundle up and head out, then she started humming softly to herself while she picked up the dishes and cleaned the kitchen for Emma.

She had no family of her own, her mom died when she was very young and she never even knew who her father was. She grew up in a series of foster homes, but now, with Gabriel and the Devereaux', Hannah felt a part of them, like she belonged, as she never had before. They had all come to mean a great deal to her.

"But, why didn't you take me with you?" Annie asked.

Tim could hear the emotion in her voice and regretted that he was having this conversation over the phone rather than in person.

"Annie, it still isn't safe for you to be anywhere other than where you are right now. You know that and I won't be gone long, just a day or two. Scott and Emma will look after you, there's nothing to worry about."

"Emma is absorbed with her baby and I don't think Scott likes me. I feel uncomfortable here. The only time that I don't feel out of place is when I'm with you."

Tim hesitated, he thought she was spot on about both Emma and Scott but felt the need to downplay it and reassure her.

"You need a safe place right now while Rufus and I try to find Jason. As soon as we do, you can have your normal life back. Isn't that what you want?"

"I do, but," her voice was so soft that he could barely hear her.

"But what?"

"What happens to us then?" she asked, and he felt a little emotion of his own rise to the surface.

"We'll figure all that out. We can talk about everything when I get back. You just stay put until then, alright? I can't do what I have to do if I'm also worried about you."

"I will, as long as it's no more than two days."

"Deal, come hell or high water, I will head home at the end of two days. I've got to go now. I'm just pulling into the parking lot."

"Stay safe."

"I will, you do the same."

He disconnected the phone and a few minutes later was knocking on the door to Rufus' motel room.

"Good to see you, man," Rufus said, as he scanned the parking lot and then shut and locked the flimsy door behind them.

"You, too. How are you holding up?"

The cuts on his grizzled face were healing, but the scars would always be visible. He could no longer shave properly on that side of his face and a scruffy gray beard was beginning to sprout around the fibrous tissues on his cheeks and chin.

He'd been in the business since Scott and Tim were just kids and it was obvious his encounter with the shifter had taken a toll on him. He looked exhausted and his pale blue eyes were red-rimmed and watery.

"I'm fine, mainly just pissed off. I can't find hide nor hair of the bastard."

Tim walked over to the city map that Rufus had taped to the cheap, paneled wall. There were several small, red circles with lines drawn between them.

"What's this?"

"It's how I found him the first time. I marked each of the murders and they all occurred in the vicinity of this park. I figured that was the hunting ground where he would disable them and then he'd drag them into a nearby alley to finish them off."

"What's his purpose?"

"He seems to be eating pieces of them, usually their hearts or other major organs."

"So that he can transform into them?"

Rufus raised a brow and squeezed his lips together tightly as he stared at the map.

"Maybe, but I don't get it. Can he store that kind of thing and change into them at another time? 'Cause he ain't changing into them right away. He was still looking like the same guy that started this spree a month ago."

"There is so much that we don't know about shifters. It really puts us at a disadvantage."

"I know, Nathan and Polly are working on that very subject as we speak. But they need a specimen to really dig into the genetics and shifters just ain't that easy to find."

"How did you finally track this one down?"

"Like I said, I thought it was the park where he was hunting, so I scoped it out."

"But how did you get on to him to begin with?" Tim asked. "Usually, we don't get that close because they look like humans and the cops just put the death down as another unsolved homicide, right?"

"True," Rufus replied. "I wasn't one hundred percent sure it was a shifter, but with the missing body parts, I knew it was something I needed to look into."

"Shifters don't usually stay long in the same area, do they?"

"No, but for some reason this guy did. Usually, they're hit and run artists, but for some reason, this one seemed partial to this location. When I saw this guy hit the park two nights in a row, he jumped onto my radar. Particularly after a body was found after the second night.

I should have followed him back to his place that night, but he didn't act at all suspicious and I didn't know about the body until the next day."

There were a couple of blurry pictures up along the side of the map, the man was not as tall as Tim, maybe around six feet. He was wearing a parka which hid most of his body, and he had thick, dark hair.

The picture wasn't clear enough to pick out many specific details on his face, but Tim was fairly certain that it was the same guy from the hospital.

"That's him?"

"Yeah, I grabbed a couple of pictures a few nights later when he came back. That night I did follow him, but I think he was on to me and left the park after just a short time. I laid way back and managed to follow him to his apartment building."

"Is that the night you went after him?"

"No, I waited. I wanted to be sure it was the right guy and was confident of it when he headed for the park again the next night. I saw him walking, very deliberately, towards a woman with a dog on a leash. The dog turned and went ballistic when the guy got close and it made him hesitate."

"Was that during the day?"

"No, it was nighttime, but they have all sorts of lighting throughout the park for the holidays. It's practically as bright as day in there. So light, in fact, that I saw his fingers turn to claws as moved towards her.

I was just about to sprint over to stop him, but it was a big dog and when it started snarling and snapping at him, the girl could hardly restrain it. Of course, she was only using one hand, she aimed some pepper spray in the guy's direction with the other one, so he stopped short and let her go on ahead."

Tim's brow was furrowed as he considered the dog's reaction to the shifter and his thoughts couldn't help returning to Callie's, and even Tolstoy's, response to Annie.

The only plausible explanations that he could up with were that they could still smell the shifter on Annie's clothes or maybe even on her body, or it could simply be that they were picking up on her irrational fear of dogs.

"What happened next?" he asked.

"I stayed way back and watched him make his way to his apartment, guess he decided to give up the hunt for the rest of the night. It never occurred to me that he might have a date.

I watched where the light went on when he entered and knew which apartment was his. I waited for a couple of hours and then decided to make my move. I never saw the girl show up and had no idea she was in there."

Again, Tim considered his words and tried to find the logical explanation, but it eluded him just now.

"Want to do a little B and E, check out his apartment?"

"Sure, now?"

"We can scope it out and if it's quiet, we might want to try it now, otherwise, it might be smarter to go this evening, after dark."

"Excellent," Scott said with a wide grin, as the last of the four snowmobiles in the barn started up easily.

"Where did you get all these, anyway?" Gabriel asked, as he walked around, running his fingers over them one by one.

They were all older models of varying sizes and manufacturers, but they still looked like they were in decent shape.

"We got them at an estate sale a couple of months ago. And I am man enough to admit that, although I never in my life anticipated even going to an estate sale, it was fun and very lucrative. And I may even do it again, not soon, but some day."

"Were they running when you got 'em?"

"No, actually, I had to do a little work on each of them to get them back on track, so to speak. None of them were in bad shape, just some odds and ends needed to replaced or repaired, or just cleaned up."

"What do you think of the woman you got staying with you?" Gabriel asked, filled with curiosity about Annie. "Will she be here long?"

"I don't know. As long as we need to be sure she's safe, I guess. But, she's kind of an odd duck and I'm not sure she'll fit in."

"What do you mean?" Gabriel asked, carefully watching everything that Scott was doing, as he wiped off the dipstick and slid it back down into the oil reservoir.

Scott looked over the engine one last time while he tried to put his feelings about Annie into words. "Hand me that wrench, would you?"

"Sure."

"Thanks," Scott said, grabbing it out of Gabriel's hand and bending over the engine once again.

"Annie's different, very close-mouthed, and no one, other than maybe Tim, knows much about her. She doesn't come downstairs and spend any time with us unless Tim is there. He seems to think a lot of her but the jury's still out as far as I'm concerned, and Emma, as well, I believe."

"Is she something non-human?" Gabriel asked. Scott picked up on the unnatural break in his voice, as if he was afraid to actually say those words out loud.

"I don't think so," Scott replied. Until he figured out how he was going to confirm what Annie actually was, one way or another, he wasn't going to fill Gabriel's head with thoughts of anything paranormal.

There was also the possibility that he was overreacting as far as Annie was concerned, and he had no problem explaining that perspective to Gabriel.

"Sometimes, I struggle to remember that people run the gamut as far as types of personalities and the way they behave. I sometimes tend to look for creatures where there aren't any. I find that's the safest route to travel so that I can avoid being caught unprepared.

However, I don't think that's the case with Annie. I'm keeping an eye on her but, at this point, I think it's just that her personality doesn't mesh with mine, or Emma's."

"I haven't met her yet but if I notice anything off, I'll be sure to let you know.

"Thanks," Scott replied, as he lowered the hood back into place.

"Maybe you can show me how to work on these kinds of things sometime. My dad left when I was young, and I never did learn anything about engines and such."

"Sure, you're going to be the man here when I'm off on a job, so you'll have to be familiar with how to repair all kinds of equipment," Scott said, trying to appear nonchalant about his response.

The kid didn't have it easy growing up, that was obvious and, even though Scott sometimes ran out of patience with him, he genuinely liked Gabriel and now considered both he and Hannah as a part of the family.

"Did you check the generator?" Scott's voice was a little gruffer than he intended, but his emotions kept bubbling up to the surface lately and he wasn't sure why.

For now, he'd blame it on the baby, or maybe the holidays. Whatever it was, he hoped he'd be back to his old curmudgeonly self again soon.

"Not yet, I filled up the gas cans last week and meant to top it off, but I forgot."

"No worries, why don't you do that now and I'll get these all covered up again."

The generator was secured from vandals and the weather in a plastic and steel storage shed just off to the side of the front doors and Gabriel headed out that way.

"Holy shit balls!" he exclaimed just a few seconds later.

Scott dropped the sled cover and sprinted toward the front of the barn, slowing down when he saw Gabriel standing just inside the open doors, looking off to the side with one hand over his heart, as if trying to keep it from jumping out of his chest.

"What's going on?" Scott asked.

"I didn't know you got a cat. It scared the crap out of me."

Scott followed his gaze and saw a large black cat, its back was arched and a low growl vibrated in its chest as it glared from one man to the other.

Its eyes were a golden-brown color and appeared to be almost glowing.

"I never saw it before," Scott said. "Maybe it's feral and is looking for some shelter from the storm that's coming."

"I suppose so. I usually like cats, but this one seems just plain wicked."

The low growl continued, and its long black tail was violently swishing back and forth.

"Well, I don't particularly care for cats but, if it wants to pull its weight and keep the vermin out of the barn, I got no problem with that, so it can stay if it wants to."

The cat seemed to understand what he was saying because the tail stopped whipping back and forth and the growl was quieting, as well.

"Creepy," Scott said, with an involuntary shudder. "Go top off the generator if it needs it. I'll finish up with the sleds and we can get out of here."

"Can I bring it a bowl of milk before I leave today?"

"Sure, the barn's yours to manage, you can do it anyway that you see fit."

"Thanks, Scott. Hannah and I can pick some things up for it on the way home."

"Don't feed it so much that it doesn't want to hunt, alright? It's going to have to earn its keep."

"Gotcha," Gabriel replied, smiling to himself as he made his way out to the check on the generator.

CHAPTER 9

The sun had just set when Tim and Rufus jimmied the front door of Jason's apartment and slipped in under the police tape crossing it. They'd come by earlier, but the area was busy with foot traffic and they would have been too noticeable when as broke in.

It was a nondescript place, the furniture was generic and the only item of note was the over-sized television hanging from the wall.

Some of the furniture had been broken during the fight and was still lying around in pieces on the cheap carpet and there were several bullet holes in the walls near the couch.

The two men checked papers they found lying around and while Rufus looked through each and every drawer in the kitchen, Tim made his way to the one bedroom. He opened the closet door and found nothing other than a few pair of dress pants and shirts in it. Other than underclothes and socks, Tim found nothing in the dresser drawers when he rummaged through them.

He wasn't sure what he was looking for, but the image of Annie kept popping into his mind and he felt fairly certain she must have kept at least a few personal items here at the apartment.

But he found nothing feminine, no clothing, no items in the bathroom that were exclusively for a woman's use, and there was only one toothbrush.

"What's up? You look perplexed," Rufus asked, as he took a step inside the bedroom.

"I know Annie had been seeing him awhile, I guess it's just strange that she didn't have any of her stuff here. You said the lights were all off when you followed him home, right?"

"Yep."

"Could she have come in and you didn't notice? Or maybe come in from a different entrance?"

"Could be, I can't say for sure. What's the interest?"

"I guess that I just find it odd, that's all. I hate unanswered questions."

"Shifter may not have wanted any of her stuff here. I think when they get ready to run, they don't want anything left behind to lead a hunter to them. He just got unlucky by me popping in unexpectedly."

"Yeah, you're probably right. Did you find anything to give us an idea where he might have headed?"

"Not a thing, he's good. Got a damn paper-shredder and not one piece of paper left intact anywhere I could find."

"We can canvas the park and see if he comes back."

"It's probably not likely but let's give it a try. I've been trying to figure out who owns the building, once I do that, I'll check in with the apartment manager, see if they have a forwarding address. If not, it's back to the drawing board."

"What do you mean?"

"Have to wait for him to start killing again and then I can follow the bodies. Rotten way to have to do it, but there's not really any other option."

They wandered around the park for a couple of hours but there was no one about on this frigid evening. The wind was picking up and snow was in the air, and no one wanted to be caught in the middle of the park once the storm started.

The snow was just beginning to fall in earnest the next morning when Tim pulled out of the motel lot and headed back home. He was frustrated that they hadn't gotten any idea of where the shifter might be, but knew they would get him eventually, they always did.

Although Tim was aware that the situation at Scott and Emma's was not ideal for Annie, and that he may have to consider putting her up in a hotel somewhere if it didn't improve soon, he was pleased that he would have a little more time to spend with her.

"Stop worrying so much. You are doing fine, just make sure you support his head."

Emma tried not to giggle as she watched the expression on Scott's face go from panic to almost total concentration as he focused completely on the task at hand, which was holding his son safely and securely.

As excited and proud as he was, the little one still scared him because he had no clue what to do with it. And it was so tiny that he worried it would slip right out of his hands if he wasn't careful.

Leaving Scott to his own devices for a few minutes, Emma went to stare out the kitchen window. It had been snowing pretty steadily since the middle of the night and they now had several inches on the ground.

The evergreen trees formed a natural border to the outer edge of their lawn and their limbs were hanging low, covered with the heavy, wet snow.

It was a pretty picture and so appropriate that it happened now, right before Christmas. Her thoughts were interrupted when she saw Tim come around the corner to the back door. A blast of cold air accompanied him as he entered, and he shut it quickly when he saw Scott trying to block the wind from hitting Brian.

"Sorry," he said, stomping the excess snow from his boots onto the mat in front of the door.

"Hello, Tim," Emma said. "How was the drive?"

"A little hairy in some spots because of the visibility but, overall, the roads weren't that bad."

He took off his gloves and stuffed them in the pockets of his wool coat, which he hung on the coat tree.

"Do you have any coffee? It did take a bit longer than it should have and I'm a little whipped."

"I'll grab you a cup, have a seat."

"Well, look at you, Dad, you're getting pretty good at that."

Scott still had a bit of a 'deer in the headlight' look on his face, but he was going to brave this out. He couldn't let his brother see how inept he felt.

"Of course, it's no big thing for me to hold my son."

Emma set the coffee on the table in front of Tim and sat down, but it was almost as if Brian sensed that she was near and started fussing, which quickly escalated into loud squalls of discontent.

With wide eyes, Scott met Emma's gaze. She tried to hold back her smile but wasn't completely successful.

"Why don't you let me hold him for now?" she said, and Scott gratefully acquiesced.

Letting out a loud breath of relief, Scott refilled his own cup and turned to his brother. "What's the scoop?"

"Not much to report," he replied. "Oh, good morning, Annie."

"You're back," she said, a wide smile on her face as she stepped into the kitchen.

"Callie," Emma said sharply, as the dog let loose a low growl from her bed over in the corner.

The smile dropped from Annie's face and she stayed frozen in her spot over near the entrance to the kitchen.

"Scott, would you mind putting Callie over into our part of the house?"

He had a contemplative look on his face as his gaze moved from Annie to Callie and back again.

Scott didn't reply to Emma's request, but he got up and grabbed Callie's collar and led her into the other room, then he closed the door that separated the kitchen from their personal quarters and returned to the table.

By then Annie had grabbed a cup of coffee and was sitting close to Tim at the table.

"You're just in time," Tim said. "I'm about to give my update, although there is not all that much to share."

The golden brown in Annie's hazel eyes glowed affectionately as she stared at Tim, and both Scott and Emma could see how strongly she felt about him.

And from the relaxed and pleased look on his face, Tim returned those feelings.

"Did you find him?"

Tim shook his head. "Nope, no sign of him at all. We scoped out his apartment, but there was nothing there to indicate where he might have gone."

"What happens now? Do I go home?"

"We don't know if he left town or not, it's probably still not safe. Rufus stayed and he's trying to track down the property manager."

"Why?"

"Jason would have had to fill out an application to rent the apartment, there might be some information in that which could help us track him down."

"Is that all you did while you were there?" Scott asked.

"We checked out the park, too, but with the snow starting, it was pretty much empty and a complete bust."

"I'd better go change him," Emma said, as Brian's squalls became louder and more persistent.

"I'll go with you," Scott said.

But, before he could escape from the kitchen, Annie called out to him and he stopped short, turning back to see what she wanted.

"Scott, I just wanted to thank you, and Emma, for continuing to let me stay here. I know that our personalities don't always mesh, but I hope you'll be patient with me."

Scott was struck by the fact that her words mirrored his very own from the day before but, rather than taking that as a sign that they were on the same page, he wondered if perhaps she had snuck out to the barn and listened in on his conversation with Gabriel.

But that couldn't be, there would have been nowhere for her to hide within hearing range. If she was there, he would have seen her. Scott continued to frown in her direction though, he never had been a believer in coincidences.

Tim and Annie were both staring at him curiously, so he smiled, and said, "Not a problem. If there is anything you need, let us know."

Scott hurried out of the kitchen, feeling even more uneasy about Annie now. But he also knew that he would have to tread lightly because, although each day he became more suspicious of Annie, at the same time, Tim was becoming more enamored of her and would only take offense to any of Scott's concerns.

He could not recall anything that had pitted he and his brother on such opposite sides of an issue before.

Scott also had more questions that he needed answered from Tim about the shifter, but the additional information could wait. He would get it another time when Annie wasn't around.

"Are you doing alright?" Tim asked, his brow furrowed as he watched his brother walk away. "Did something happen with Scott? Is that why you said that to him?"

"Oh, no, I can tell he doesn't feel comfortable with me. It's a strange situation because I have to live in his house. And, don't get me wrong, I really appreciate it. I just wish I knew how to get along better with him and Emma."

"Grab your coat and boots. It really is beautiful outside, let's take a walk and talk about this some more."

Annie had a doubtful look on her face as she stared out the kitchen window but shrugged her shoulders and did as he asked. A few minutes later they were wandering through the woods, kicking snow out of their way as they trudged slowly through the winter wonderland.

"So, you didn't find out anything of interest on your trip?" she asked.

"Not really. Do you mind if I ask you a personal question, though?"

"You can ask but I might not answer," Annie replied.

Tim bit his lip to keep from smiling at her response, it was precisely that attitude that continued to surprise and impress him as he got to know her better.

"When we checked out Jason's apartment, there was nothing of yours there. I just thought it was strange because you said you'd been together a few months, right?"

She lifted an eyebrow as she stared into his face. "Why is that a concern?"

"I guess I'm just curious about the extent of your relationship."

"You mean were we having sex? And if we were, why didn't I keep my stuff there for when we spent the night together?"

Tim felt a little foolish hearing his questions voiced out loud. "I'm sorry, none of that is my business."

She stared hard at him and then turned away, trying to decide what, if anything she would share with him.

"We only went out for about six months," she began slowly. "I told you before that I have had some bad luck with men in the past, right?"

"Yes," he replied, "but you don't have to explain anything to me."

"I want to," she said, refusing to meet his eyes as she stared straight ahead.

They continued on in silence while she collected her thoughts. The snow was still falling steadily around them and it deadened any other noise, making it easy to imagine that they were the only people currently populating the world.

"I was only ten years old when my mom and dad died in a car accident. I was in the car, too, but I lived and they didn't. After that, I went to live with my grandmother. She was a hard woman and I think she blamed me for their deaths for some reason.

I left there as soon as I was old enough to work and earn a living. Over the next few years, I managed to get myself into even more abusive situations."

Tim couldn't help but notice how she glossed over the abuse that she suffered at her grandmother's hands, which allowed his imagination to run free, and a deep fury burned inside him at the thought of the things that she might have gone through.

Annie shuddered as she continued to recall some of the uglier moments in her past, but continued her story in a flat, emotionless voice. "I'm a little leery of people in general, particularly men, and I've been trying to learn from my mistakes."

"How so?"

"I've stopped rushing into every situation with my eyes closed and fingers crossed that everything will work out perfectly. I was trying so desperately to find the right person, the one that would finally love me, that I was ignoring certain glaring problems with them until it was too late. Now, I try to slow things down, make sure of what I'm dealing with before I go all in."

Tim felt relieved and wasn't sure why, he thought maybe because more and more, it didn't appear that Annie had actually ever been in love with Jason.

The more time that he spent with Annie and learned what made her tick, the more he found himself wanting to take her into his arms and keep her safe, to bring her all the happiness that she deserved, but had never been able to attain.

Annie gave Tim a sidelong glance and he could see the smile on her face. "That's the long answer to your question. We had not had sex yet and I've never spent the entire night with him, that's why none of my stuff was at his apartment."

"Thank you for explaining, but you didn't have to share all of that with me."

"I wanted to. I know you have good intentions and I want you to understand why I am so stand-offish at times, particularly with Scott and Emma. I appreciate what they are doing for me, I just can't relax around them like I can with you."

"You know that you don't have to stay here, right?"

"What do you mean? Do you want me to leave?"

She stopped walking and turned towards him, her eyes wide with confusion.

"Of course not, I just don't want you to feel uncomfortable. I can get you a hotel room if you'd prefer."

His brown eyes softened when he saw the look of relief appear on her face. Annie looked up at Tim and the fat, wet snowflakes melted as they hit her cheeks.

There was something almost destitute in the look she gave him and it tugged at Tim's heart. All of the women that he had relationships with in the past were strong and self-reliant. Annie was different than all of them.

She was strong in her own way, but her strength was buried somewhere deep inside of her. From the outside looking in, she seemed fragile and ready to break if even one more trauma occurred in her life. Annie was completely alone, except for a grandmother that apparently was not at all kind to her.

Tim wanted nothing more than to help her, to show her that he was here for her, but he wasn't sure how to do that without scaring her away.

He pulled Annie into his arms, struggling to embrace both her and her heavy parka as he leaned down.

Her cold, full lips parted in anticipation and he kissed her long and hard, pulling her up as tightly as possible against his body, savoring the feel of her in his arms.

They stayed that way for several minutes, enjoying the taste and the touch of one another, but the snowflakes were coming down thicker now and melting down the back of Tim's neck. He shivered and pulled away from her.

"Shall we head back?"

"Sure," she replied. Tim noticed how flushed her cheeks were and was fairly certain it wasn't just because of the cold.

They slowly started back, following what was left of their own tracks but, after a few short moments, Tim stopped suddenly and turned in a full circle, staring hard into the dense trees.

"What are you looking for?" Annie asked, seeing the set look on his face.

"There are new tracks over ours," he replied, still scanning the trees around them.

"Someone was following us?"

"No," he replied, "it looks like a large dog, maybe a coyote. The snow has filled in most of the tracks, but it looks big, heavy, almost like a wolf, but we don't have wolves in this area."

Annie grabbed his sleeve. "Come on, let's get out here, please."

Tim knew how frightened she was of dogs, so the thought of a wolf being in the area must be almost paralyzing to her. He grabbed her hand and the two of them hurried along back to the house.

The black wolf stayed hidden in the heavy copse of fir trees and watched them hurry away. There was a low, constant growl emanating from its chest as it struggled with indecision.

Anger was crowding its thoughts and making it difficult to tamp down the bloodlust that was threatening to break loose. It held back long enough for Tim and Annie to get out of sight, then let out a vicious snarl and turned away, heading back towards the road.

There was very little traffic and it was loping easily along the edge of the roadway, veering off into a dirt turn off down the road.

It was an access road to a cell tower and was rarely used. There was a car parked behind a line of trees, hidden from the road, and the wolf headed straight for it.

As he did so, his body began to morph, and Jason Turnbull silently suffered the pain of changing once again. When he was young, the agony had sometimes been overpowering, but he'd been through it hundreds of times since then and now felt only a mild discomfort.

When the change was complete, however, the frigid cold on his skin was intolerable. He jumped inside the car and quickly started the engine, blasting the heat while he tried to control his shivering.

Jason couldn't get the picture of what he had witnessed between Annie and Tim out of his mind and replayed it over and over while he put on the clothes that he'd left folded neatly on the passenger seat of the car.

Although his skin was still cold, his blood boiled when he pictured their lips meeting and saw his Annie being held tightly in Tim's arms.

Now fully human, he still let loose a wicked snarl when he thought of what he was going to do to Tim, he just wished it could be sooner, rather than later.

He would take his Annie back from them, but not yet, not until he was sure that he could do so successfully. They were hunters and he would not underestimate them under any circumstances.

For now, he would just continue to watch. When the time was right, he would strike with everything that he had and if there were no survivors, other than Annie, of course, that would be just fine with him.

CHAPTER 10

It continued to snow, off and on, until late the next day. Tim stayed at the house with them and he and Annie spent a lot of their time talking quietly or playing games together.

He was grateful that she had told him all she had about herself and he respected her desire to take her time, although his body didn't always necessarily agree.

They would make out sometimes, upstairs in the sitting room or in her bedroom, but no more than that. Although he sometimes found it difficult to restrain himself, Tim wasn't going to push Annie into doing something that she wasn't ready to do.

By the middle of the week, the snow had stopped completely, and Tim decided to run home to look in on his mother and check with Rufus while he was there.

"Gabriel is on his way over," Scott said, finally tracking down Emma in the nursery. "He said he had some more lights to put up on the outside of the house. I'll help with that, so he doesn't hurt anything, including himself."

"Scott, be nice, he does so much for us."

"I know, I'm kidding." He kissed Emma's forehead and continued. "Once he's done, we're going to take the sleds and make some trails through the woods. We may even find a place for some jumps."

"Seriously?"

"Your boys will love it. I want them to really enjoy themselves."

"They can do that without breaking any bones. Hey, what about that wolf or dog that Tim was telling you about. Are you going to look for that?"

"I almost forgot about it. I'll bring my pistol, just in case, but whether it was a wolf, a coyote or a dog, it's unlikely it'll still be in the area. The storm must have pushed it through."

"How can you say that for sure?"

"Well, I can't, but I haven't seen any tracks around the house, so it certainly hasn't been close by. You have nothing to worry about but I'll keep my eyes peeled for it, alright?"

"Fine," she replied, with a quick kiss on his lips before he headed outside. "I'm seriously bored and think I'll make a quick trip into town."

"Be careful driving and we already have more than enough presents for everyone."

"I know," she replied with a giggle. "I'll try to restrain myself from picking up anymore."

"Good, I'll see you later."

Gabriel pulled up just as Scott was making his way out to the barn.

"Wearing that fancy new hat again, are you?" Scott asked, once Gabriel caught up to him.

"It really keeps me warm, man, you should get one."

"Maybe, not sure it's my style though. So, let me make sure I've got two sleds gassed up and then we can do whatever you wanted to do with the lights before we head out, does that work?"

"Sure, hey, have you seen that cat around?"

"No," Scott said, his brow furrowed. "I forgot all about it. Weren't you feeding it?"

"I brought food every day since then and left it when I couldn't find the cat, but it's hasn't eaten any of it."

"Well, maybe it was just running ahead of the storm. Or maybe the wolf got it."

"What wolf?" Gabriel asked, with a nervous tremor in his voice.

"I'm just kidding, Tim saw some tracks a few days ago, probably a big dog."

"Right around here?"

"No, in the woods, nowhere near the house, or the barn, so your cat is probably fine."

"Gee whiz," Gabriel replied, "I hope so."

Annie had been spending most of her time in her room or with Tim, although she would occasionally come down to the Great Room to grab a book to read or to watch a movie.

She was very quiet, and Emma hardly knew she was about. Although she and Scott couldn't help but have their suspicions about Annie, they'd found no definitive proof that she was anything other than a troubled woman who had gotten caught up in a nightmare that was not of her own making.

Emma hadn't spent much time getting to know her and now that she was getting back to normal, she felt a little guilty about that. Annie was alone with strangers and the holidays were coming up soon. Emma felt that the least that she could do would be to reach out and make an effort to get to know Annie a little better.

She made her way to the Great Room and found Annie relaxing there with a book. The girl jumped up nervously when she entered.

"I'm sorry, I didn't mean to startle you."

"It's alright," Annie said, lowering her gaze as her face flushed guiltily for some reason.

"My kids will be here on Friday and I thought I'd run into town and pick up some groceries and maybe some last minute gifts. Would you like to go with me?"

Annie hesitated, she did not particularly care for Emma's company, however, there really was very little to do and she was sick and tired of just sitting around, so she nodded her head.

"Great," Emma said, "meet me in the kitchen in about ten minutes and we can head out."

The Town of Edgewater was only about fifteen minutes away so there was very little small talk on the drive in. Emma took her Mustang and had Brian secured in a carseat in the back. She was thankful that Scott had put the snow tires on for her because after this recent storm, the roads were still a little slick.

It took almost as long to find an available parking spot in town as it had to drive there, but eventually they managed to do so.

"We can pick up groceries last," Emma said, as she unbuckled Brian from the car seat and tried to adjust him in her arms along with her large purse, which was doubling as a diaper bag for this trip. "Is there any place in particular you'd like to check out?"

"No, thank you. Tim brought me here the other day and we went to all the little shops."

"Good, I'm glad you got to see them. Brian ate just before we left so we are probably safe for a couple of hours before I have to worry about him wanting to eat again. We can just window shop along this main stretch, if you'd like. The store that I need to go to is down on the next block."

"That's fine," Annie said, walking slowly alongside Emma.

"I wanted to apologize to you," Emma said, as they started down the sidewalk.

The walks had all been shoveled and salted but there were a few slippery spots so Emma had to watch where she was walking to be doubly sure of her footing since she didn't want to take a chance of falling with Brian in her arms.

"For what?"

"I haven't been a very good host and you've been pretty much left to entertain yourself. But I'm starting to feel like myself again, so I hope we can spend more time together."

Emma did lift her gaze over to Annie at that point and was surprised at the blank look on her face, as if neither the apology nor the offer meant anything whatsoever to her.

"I've been fine taking care of myself," Annie replied.

It was not exactly the response that Emma expected. She was beginning to think the problem between them may not have been because she hadn't been herself lately, after all. Maybe the problem had been Annie all along.

"Tell me more about yourself," Emma said, struggling to find a way to actually engage with this woman.

"There isn't much to tell. I work in a dentist's office and process the insurance claims. Not very exciting, is it?"

"Well, I'm sure there must be something redeeming about it," Emma replied. "What about your family?"

"I don't really have anyone. Jason was pretty much the only person in my life until all that went to hell. How about you, have you and Scott been married a long time?"

"No," Emma replied. "Believe it or not, we just got married in the summer. We first met several years ago but didn't get back together until earlier this year. Since then, everything has happened in a whirlwind. It's been pretty fast-moving, to say the least."

"So, you haven't lived in this area for long?"

"No, we just bought the house a couple of months ago."

"And, what about family?"

"I have three children."

"What about Scott?"

"What about him?" Emma asked.

"Does he have a lot of family?"

Annie's persistent questions were starting to raise some red flags and Emma began to get uncomfortable. She stopped walking and turned to meet Annie's eyes.

"His mother, why are you so curious about our families?"

"I was only trying to make conversation. Did I say something wrong?"

"No, you're fine," Emma replied, but that was not what she actually believed. The questions were innocent enough, but Emma felt like she was giving away information that she shouldn't, although that made no sense. It wasn't as if she was sharing state secrets.

The one other thing that consistently bothered Emma was Annie's facial expression, which always seemed to appear blank and never showed any emotion, regardless of the circumstances or the conversation.

In truth, the only emotion that Emma had noticed on Annie's face was in response to being around Tim. So, obviously, she did possess the ability. Maybe she truly was damaged and just had trouble showing her emotions to people she wasn't comfortable with.

The women's eyes met, Emma's were a suspicious green and Annie's a cold hazel color. A man pushed past Annie on the sidewalk and almost knocked her off her feet. Emma wasn't sure, but thought she heard Annie actually hiss at him as he continued on his way.

"Are we done?" Annie asked, after she regained her composure and turned back towards Emma.

"The bake shop is just ahead on our left. Cookie day is Saturday, so I want to make sure I have everything we'll need. It won't take long."

Annie helped carry the bags back to the car a short time later and they were home in no time. There was not much conversation on the way back and Emma couldn't say it with any certainty but, for some reason, it felt like their tenuous relationship was now even rockier than it was before they left.

"Oh, look at that," Emma said, as they pulled up the driveway.

"What?"

"The cupola," Emma said.

"I don't know what that is," Annie replied.

"It's that square, dome-like structure on top of the roof. Gabriel said he was going to finish decorating and he must have done that while we were gone.

He did a great job with the garland and lights. Look at the huge red bell hanging in the center of it. It looks so festive and beautiful. I love a lot of colorful lights during the holidays, don't you?"

Emma had stopped the car as she checked out the new decorations and turned towards Annie, whose face remained emotionless.

"It looks wonderful," Annie said, but her voice was flat, and she was obviously not impressed.

Scott heard them pull up and met them in the garage. He started unloading the bags from the car while Emma grabbed Brian, who was just beginning to wake up.

Annie continued to sit in the passenger side seat and Emma bent down towards her, and asked, "Is everything alright?"

"Will you get your dog out of here so I can go into the house?"

"Sure, she'll come in with us, but you really don't have to worry about Callie."

Annie just stared at Emma with a set jaw and narrowed eyes.

"Come on, Callie," Emma said, as she and Scott made their way along the breezeway and into the kitchen.

"You can leave those on the table, Scott," Emma said, "I'll take care of them later, it's just cookie stuff. Will you take Callie to our room and I'll be right in."

Brian was starting to fuss more now, but she waited for Annie to come inside and, as Emma was hanging up her coat, she said, "Annie, I really appreciate you coming with me today. I hope we can spend more time and get know each other better."

"Me, too," Annie replied, pasting an obviously fake smile onto her face. "Thanks for taking me along."

Annie headed up to her room and Emma hurried into their bedroom.

"What the matter?" Scott asked, seeing the look on her face.

Emma set Brian on the changing table and started pulling him out of his snowsuit, but she turned her head to meet Scott's eyes.

"There is something completely off with that woman, but I can't put my finger on exactly what it is."

"What happened?"

"Nothing really, she was just asking all kinds of questions about you and me and our families and how long we've been here. It just felt wrong. And she's cold, Scott."

"What do you mean?"

"Emotionless. She'll say something nice but there is no feeling in her words, her eyes or her facial expressions. It's bizarre."

"You're describing a sociopath, or a psychopath."

Emma's hands froze in place and Scott could see the fear on her face.

"Don't freak out, Emma. I'm pretty sure that's not the case with Annie." He moved over closer to her side. "You need to tell me, though, how concerned are you? I agree with what you said, and she rubs me the wrong way, as well. Then there's Callie, I really don't like the way she reacts to Annie. I can ask her to leave if you'd like."

As she quietly thought over Scott's offer, Emma turned back towards the baby and carefully finished removing the snowsuit, then his other clothing so she could change him.

"I'm not afraid of her. I don't think we have to worry in that sense. And it's so close to Christmas, how can we justify kicking her out when she could be in danger just because she made me a little uncomfortable. Besides, your brother seems to be able to see something in her that we don't. If she really is a psycho, wouldn't he know that?"

"Hard to say, you damn women have a way of wrapping us around your little fingers and we can't see what's in front of our face."

He waggled his finger in front of the baby's face and laughed out loud at Brian's expression.

"We'll keep a close eye on her and, Emma," he said seriously, "you say the word and she's gone, understand? You don't have to worry about Annie. I'll pay for a motel if I have to."

"Even if your brother never speaks to you again because if it?"

"Even then."

"Alright, you have a deal. Thank you."

Jason had followed Emma and Annie as they made their way along the streets of Edgewater, although neither of them realized it.

Fortunately, the sidewalks were crowded and they never bothered to look behind them. He was able to stay close enough to overhear their conversation but learned very little that was of any help. He considered just grabbing Annie and taking off, he missed her and wanted her back in his life. But, then he would not have fulfilled his entire mission and would only have given the hunters a heads up about his being nearby, so he had to restrain himself, for at least a little longer.

When the burly man with no manners walked into Annie and almost caused her to fall, Jason could feel his body beginning to change in response and had to stop following them at that point.

Normally, he would consciously make himself change but, occasionally, when his emotions were strong, that could trigger a change, as well. To stop it from happening, he headed down a small alleyway and took several deep breaths, clenching and unclenching his hands as he tried to regain control of himself.

Once he had done that he hurried back out onto the sidewalk. Annie and Emma were no longer in sight, but far up ahead was the burly man, and Jason set his sights on him.

The man was taller and broader than most of the other people out and about and was easy to follow from a distance. He stopped only once to go inside a liquor store and Jason pretended to window shop until the man walked back outside with his brown paper bag filled with liquid gold.

There was a bounce to the man's step now, he was obviously looking forward to going somewhere and spending the rest of his day getting thoroughly drunk.

Most of the houses in town were large and expensive but, hidden down on the south side there were a few back streets where the homes were small and not very well maintained. The burly man made his way into one of them and Jason stayed back, keeping an eye on the place for a time.

As the afternoon progressed, Jason moved stealthily around the small house but saw no movement, other than from the big man inside, and decided it was time to make his move.

The burly man was in a wife beater tee shirt when he opened the door in response to Jason's persistent knocking.

"What do you want?" His voice was low and rumbled out of his broad chest.

Jason was much smaller than the behemoth but didn't feel the slightest bit scared or unsure. He knew what he was capable of.

"May I come in?"

"Why?"

"I have something I need to discuss with you."

The large man stared at him in confusion, he'd already downed half the bottle of vodka and was falling into a nice, pleasant fugue-like state and wasn't sure what to do with this man at his door.

"What?"

"It's quite chilly out here, would you mind if I came inside where it's warm?"

The burly man was not at all afraid of Jason, who seemed harmless and unassuming, but he rarely had visitors and couldn't help but be suspicious of anyone that did come calling.

"It could mean some money falling into your hands."

That put a sparkle in the burly man's eyes, and he opened the door wider and welcomed Jason into his house.

"Talk," the man rumbled, as he sat down in the slightly off-kilter recliner and picked up his glass with a shaky hand.

Jason walked around the messy room, ignoring the uncleanly stench of the place as he tried to get his bearings. The burly man's name was Alan Boyd according to the unopened bill from the power company that he picked up from one of the scarred, wooden end tables.

"Leave my stuff alone," Alan said, taking a hefty drink from his glass. "Tell me what you want or get out of here."

Jason turned towards the Alan, his amber eyes boring into him. "Are we alone?"

"Of course."

"Will we remain alone or is there a chance of our being interrupted? I do not want anyone else involved with this."

Alan was getting more and more intrigued and hastened to assure Jason that they would not be interrupted. "My wife left me years ago. I live here by myself, even the dog took off on me."

He laughed out loud and it echoed off the thin walls.

"Good," Jason said, taking a step closer to him.

Perhaps some of the neighbors heard Alan's horrendous screams through those thin walls but, if they did, they chose to ignore them.

CHAPTER 11

"Back so soon?" Scott asked Emma the next day when she pulled into the garage.

"Yes, your Mom and I only had to drop off the coats for the coat drive and the toys for toy drive. She stays very involved with her community, doesn't she?"

"She always has," he replied, struggling to figure out how to unsnap Brian from the confines of the car seat. "It means a great deal to her to be able to go out and give to others that are less fortunate. Shit."

"Move out of the way. I'll get it," Emma said, trying to muffle her laughter.

"This kid stuff is a lot of work. How the hell is anyone supposed to be able to figure this crap out?" Scott asked, his voice filled with frustration.

"You're adorable," Emma replied, as she quickly unbundled Brian from his seat and turned towards Scott.

"Hello, girl," Emma said, when Callie walked over to check on her and Brian. "Is she helping you shovel the driveway?"

"I thought some fresh air would be good for her, but she's been out here awhile, you might want to take her in with you."

"Okay, will you be coming in for lunch soon?"

"I'm almost done with this, so it'll just be a few minutes."

"Good," she replied, and headed into the breezeway which would take her to the kitchen.

She set Brian on the floor in his carrier and started removing her boots and coat but stopped short in response to Callie's actions.

The dog had been gently sniffing Brian, making sure he was safe and healthy, but she suddenly froze in place and the hair on her back rose and a low growl started in her chest.

At first, Emma's heart started thumping fearfully in her chest, worried that Callie was about to attack the baby, something she would never have imagined was possible. But, then Callie turned away from Brian and towards the other side of the kitchen, the side that led to their private quarters.

Callie took a few stealthy steps in that direction and Emma quickly kicked off her last boot and followed along behind the dog. She jumped when Callie let out a sharp bark and then Emma heard a soft voice, filled with fear, coming from around the corner of the doorway.

"Will you keep that dog away from me?" Annie asked, and Emma finally allowed herself to release the breath she'd been holding.

She grabbed a leash from the coatrack and snapped it onto Callie's collar, then she stepped back away so Annie could enter the kitchen.

"I've got her, you can come in here now."

Annie peeked around the corner and glared at Callie, who was still letting loose a low growl from deep in her chest as their eyes met.

"What the hell were you doing in our private quarters?"

"I was, um," Annie hesitated, and Emma was certain she was trying to come up with a plausible lie, "I was looking for another book to read. I have nothing to do and I'm bored."

Emma's green eyes were glittering angrily, she felt almost violated by Annie's intrusion into their private space.

"Don't ever go into our private quarters again. We're going out of our way for you right now, providing you with food and a safe place to stay. The least you can do is show a little respect. Do it again and you're leaving. I don't care if that's on Christmas Day and in the middle of a blizzard, do you understand?"

"What's going on?" Scott asked, as he walked into the kitchen before Annie had a chance to respond.

"Annie apparently didn't understand what parts of the house were out of bounds for guests."

Annie looked back and forth between them, she could see their anger and knew she was walking a fine line.

"I really am sorry, I didn't mean to upset or offend you. I simply wanted a book to read, but I'll never go in there again. I promise. Are we good?"

"We're fine, as long as you remember what I just told you," Emma replied.

With a brief nod in Emma's direction, Annie hurried out of the kitchen.

"She didn't have a book in her hand," Scott noted.

"I know, maybe you'd better take a quick look around in there and make sure nothing is out of place or missing."

"I will," Scott said, kissing her forehead and then leaning down to kiss Brian's fat cheek.

Running his fingers roughly through his hair, he turned and stared out in the direction that Annie had gone.

"I want her out of here, Emma. It's getting weirder and weirder every day that she stays. But I do not know how to approach this with Tim, which is even stranger, because I've never had trouble telling him how I feel about anything. But with her, I feel like I have to walk on eggshells as far as he is concerned."

"I know," Emma said. "It's alright, the kids will be here tomorrow and then it's Christmas, so let's just put this behind us. If she is still here after Christmas, we'll have to have to a serious talk with Tim and she will be leaving then, whether he likes it or not."

"I love it when you go all Rambo," Scott said, a smile lighting his face as he left to check out their quarters.

Emma couldn't say for sure, but she thought she heard footsteps heading down the hall towards the staircase and was fairly certain that Annie had been standing just outside the doorway listening to them.

When Tim showed up a little later, he found Annie upstairs in the little sitting area, just staring into space and looking like a lost puppy.

"What's the matter?" he asked softly, sitting down beside her on the comfortable, overstuffed loveseat and taking her hands in his. No green or gold highlights shimmering in them today, just a solemn brown color which reflected her sadness.

"I screwed up," she replied, lifting her hazel eyes to meet his.

"What do you mean?"

"Didn't your brother tell you?"

"No, I think he and Emma are in their own side of the house. I came to see you, not them. What happened?"

She blew out a long breath and tried to explain. "I went into their side of the house when they weren't here. I was just looking for a book to read, Tim, I swear that's all. But they were very upset with me and,"

Her voice broke and she looked downward, trying to hide the tears that were collecting.

Tim enveloped her in his arms and cupped her head with one large hand, holding it gently against his chest, letting her tears burn through the material of his shirt.

"There's no reason to cry," he murmured, kissing the top of her head.

"I think they hate me," she whispered.

"Of course, they don't," Tim said, a bit more forcefully than necessary. "Look at me, Annie."

She lifted her head and raised her bloodshot eyes to meet his.

"Even if you overstepped a little, it's not the end of the world. Scott and Emma are highly emotionally charged right now. They've had so many things happen in their lives this year, and now the baby is here, and Emma's kids will be showing up soon.

It's all new, it's stressful and, under other circumstances, things would be very different between them and you."

"I don't know about that," Annie said. "It's not the first time that I've gotten on the wrong side of someone unintentionally."

"What do you mean?"

"I rub people the wrong way. I don't know why, maybe because I'm so closed off emotionally. I just don't play well with others."

She smiled then and her hazel eyes had a little of their sparkle back when she met Tim's.

"I like the way you play," he murmured, then moved forward, capturing her lips with his own.

Annie moaned and leaned heavily against him, savoring the feel of his lips on hers. Their hands began to explore one another and Tim slid his hands under her blouse, relishing the feel of her soft, silky skin.

"I want you," he whispered against her lips.

She pulled back away from him, her hazel eyes wide with passion. She placed a finger over his lips and held his gaze with her own as she struggled to make a decision.

"I want you, too," she said softly.

"Do I hear a but in there?" Tim asked, as disappointment ripped through him.

"You do," she said, tracing her finger over his lips, then leaning forward to place a chaste kiss upon them. "You are a special person, Tim, and if I have my druthers, we will be spending a lot more time together.

But I have to be true to myself. It was what, a week or so ago, that I was Jason? And now my life has been turned completely upside down. I don't want to be with you for the wrong reasons. I want this to be something real between us. Can you understand that?"

"Of course, I can," Tim replied, shifting uncomfortably on the loveseat, trying to keep the disappointment from showing on his face.

"Thank you," Annie replied. "I've never met anyone quite like you and I hope you can continue believing in me."

"What's not to believe in, Annie? I'm here for you, for whatever you need."

The next morning, Shelly pulled up outside with her Tiguan packed to the roof with her two brothers, numerous suitcases, Christmas gifts, and a fancy cat box with her Siamese, Smoky, inside of it.

It warmed Scott's heart to see Emma's face light up as she ran out to greet her children. He, on the other hand, wasn't sure exactly what his role was. He'd never spent much time with the kids and wasn't sure how to act, especially since they were still adjusting to the fact that he'd married their mother.

"Hi, Scott," Shelly said, seeing him hanging back inside the foyer, watching as they greeted each other and made their way into the house.

He and Tim had saved her life, as well as her friends and, although she would never admit it, they had become very important to her.

Even to the extent that she found herself looking for their traits, some of them anyway, in the guys her age that wanted to take her out. And, so far, she hadn't been at all successful in finding them.

"The house looks great," she said.

Scott had a stern look on his face as he silently watched her approach, then it creased into a smile and he opened his arms. "Thanks, come here and give me a hug."

Shelly's blonde hair was short and stylish, her dark blue eyes snapped with happiness and curiosity, and Scott knew that he would always have a warm spot in his heart for her.

He originally thought Shelly was nothing more than a spoiled brat that continuously took advantage of her mother because of the divorce but, in the short time they'd known each other, Shelly had matured in many ways and Scott really enjoyed spending time with her.

Shelly only hesitated a second and then stepped into his arms and wrapped her own around him. Shelly couldn't help feeling a little twinge of disloyalty towards her father, but forced that thought from her head.

Scott would now be playing as big a part in her adult life as her own father and she was okay with that, it just took a little getting used to.

"I'm glad you can spend some time with us," Scott said, as he released her. "You will stay for a little while, won't you?"

"Yeah, I love Christmas and I miss spending time with my brothers, and you and Mom, too," she added quickly.

There was no time for further conversation because both boys came over to greet Scott then. No hugs, but he did share a hearty handshake with each them. He had spent a little time with the two teenagers, but not much, and it was his relationship with them that he decided would need the most work while they were here.

There was a loud wail through the baby monitor and everyone immediately fell silent.

"Would you like to meet your brother?" Emma asked excitedly.

The boys were game to do so, but Shelly didn't respond, just stared down at the hardwood floor.

Emma noticed and hid the sharp pain that fluttered across her chest. "Shelly, you can come join us later if you'd like."

"Okay, I think I'll take my stuff up to my room and let Smoky out."

Emma bit the inside of her lip and then put an arm around each of her sons and led them over to the other side of the house where Brian's room was.

"You any good with babies?" Scott asked, before she headed upstairs.

"What you mean, any good?"

"Do you know what to do with them?"

"What a silly question, of course I do. I used to babysit for people all the time."

"Excellent," Scott said, "would you be able to do me a favor then?"

"Sure."

"I am completely inept with the baby. I don't even know the right way to hold him. Will you spend a little time with him and me, teach me a few things so that your mother doesn't think I'm a complete idiot?"

Shelly laughed out loud. "Of course, I can teach you a thing or two so you can save some of your pride."

"Thanks," he replied, but then stared into the cat carrier as Smoky arched her back and hissed loudly. "What's with that?"

Shelly looked down at her curiously, then Scott and Shelly both glanced up the stairway when they heard the creak of a step.

"Oh, hi, this is," Scott never quite knew how to refer to the children, but came to a decision and blurted out, "Shelly, our daughter."

Shelly looked at him with a raised eyebrow, but that sounded right, so she didn't question it.

"This is Annie," he said, as the woman in question made her way further down the stairs. "She's staying with us for a little while."

He couldn't explain anything more than that because Smoky was now letting out a horrific growl and banging against the side of her carrier.

Scott looked from the box to Annie and couldn't help but notice the coldness on her face as she stared at the cat.

"Don't you like cats either, Annie?"

She raised her slitted eyes toward him and a vein began to throb in her neck.

"Not particularly, is that thing going to be upstairs?"

"Shelly, for now, why don't you take the cat into our apartment, you can go in through the kitchen."

Shelly's face was filled with confusion, she'd never seen Smoky behave that way before, but she nodded and headed towards the other side of the house.

The hair on the back of Scott's neck was standing on end and he knew better than to ignore Callie, the cat, and his own reaction to Annie. There was a serious problem with this woman, and he couldn't just let it go anymore.

No more screwing around, it was time to figure out what her deal was before something happened that they would all regret.

The problem was how he could do that without getting his brother on board because, so far, Tim had fought the slightest suggestion that something might be amiss with her.

Scott ran his fingers roughly through his hair and his eyes narrowed as he watched Annie make her way back upstairs to her room.

He checked his watch and realized that with the kids just arriving, he didn't have time to look into this right now. But he decided it was suddenly his highest priority and he would get it taken care of as soon as he was able to do so, without anyone being the wiser.

"Mom, do you think you could leave Tolstoy home today?" Tim asked, as he watched his mother pick up the puppy's leash.

"Why? He loves to go over to Scott and Emma's and play with everyone. And the boys are there and maybe they will all tire each other out."

"It's Annie, she's afraid of him, and of Callie, of all dogs, actually."

"That's her problem then, wouldn't you say?"

"Mom, please, just for today?"

"Tolstoy is family, that girl is not. She can go to her room while we're there."

"I really don't understand why you and Scott are being such hard-asses about her," Tim said, rubbing between his eyes to ease some of his tension. "She went through some serious trauma and has issues. I get that, but can't we just give her the benefit of the doubt?"

Doris watched her son closely and was not happy when she realized just how strongly he seemed to care for the girl. Granted, she'd felt the same way about Emma initially, and ended up being wrong about her.

But that was different, Emma was married when she and Scott first met, Annie just seemed capricious. There was something off about her that Doris could not get comfortable with.

"Why is today so important?"

"Emma's kids are home and we'll be decorating the tree and doing things as a family. I just thought, since Annie has no one, that it would be good for her to share that. The dogs make her uneasy and I want it to be special for her, too."

As much as Doris mistrusted Annie, she could see how important this was to Tim and so she relented.

"I won't bring Tolstoy today, but it's the only day Annie gets. Tolstoy is a part of our family and I will not leave him home alone just because she has an irrational fear of dogs. She needs to deal with that, he's still a baby and he's never bitten anyone. Annie needs to face her fear and he's the one she should do it with."

"Thanks, Mom," Tim said with a grin, as he bent down and kissed her forehead. "I'll talk to her about that."

But Doris knew that he wouldn't even bring the subject up to her. Tim treated Annie like a fragile doll that he needed to protect, but Doris was fairly certain that the girl could handle a lot more than she let on.

CHAPTER 12

Shelly and the two boys barely had their suitcases unpacked when Gabriel and Hannah showed up, with Doris and Tim making their way into the house just a few minutes after that.

There was complete bedlam initially, as all the appropriate greetings were made, and people wandered into the Great Room to get comfortable.

"The house looks lovely, Emma," Doris said, as she slowly wandered around, examining the various Christmas decorations. "These aren't all new, are they?"

"No," Emma replied, "there were some items that I did keep when I sold the old house. I couldn't bear to get rid of the Christmas decorations. I've had many of them since the kids were young. You have your pictures and I have my Christmas decorations."

Doris understood perfectly. "Where's the little one?"

"Napping, I tried to time this so we could have an hour or so to decorate the tree before he wakes up. It's nice and full but looks so bare and lonely right now."

She and Doris glanced over at the fat tree in front of the window and Emma shook her head in dismay as Scott, Tim and Gabriel were all trying to unravel and wind the lights around the tree.

The tree itself almost tipped over as they made Gabriel slide in along the back side and operate as their liaison so they could be sure the lights went all the way around.

"Too many cooks in the kitchen," Doris murmured.

Annie did not come down to join them, although Emma had asked her if she would like to. She enlisted Hannah and Doris to help her out in the kitchen to prepare some snacks and drinks for everyone.

By the time they returned, the lights and garland were up and Scott heaved a sigh of relief when he saw the bucket of ice holding several bottles of beer.

"Merry Christmas to me," he said, lifting it in a toast to whoever was around before twisting off the cap and allowing the cool beverage to relieve his parched throat.

Tim grabbed one for himself and Gabriel, trying to fit in with the other guys, helped himself, as well. The three of them stood back, out of the way, as James, Collin and Shelly dragged the plastic tubs filled with the decorations over towards the tree.

Emma stood in front of Scott, leaning back against him, and he reached around with his free hand to snuggle her up tighter against his body.

"I feel so happy," she said quietly, unable to drag her eyes away from her three oldest children as they squabbled and fought over which ornaments would go where.

"Then so am I," Scott replied, kissing the top of her head. He leaned over a little further and whispered into her ear, "While the kids are hanging the bulbs, I'm going to try to talk some sense into Tim, okay?"

"Sure," she replied, turning in his arms and lifting herself onto her toes to softly kiss his lips. "Good luck."

Scott walked over to Tim, and asked, "Would you come out to the kitchen with me?"

"Why, forget how to get there?"

"Such a smartass you are," Scott replied. "I want to talk to you alone."

Tim suspected what the conversation would be about and felt himself tensing up and getting ready to do battle before they even sat down at the kitchen table.

"What did she do now?" he asked, his voice edgy.

"You mean, other than snooping in our personal quarters and having the cat react to her just as badly as Callie has been?"

"Annie already told me about the "snooping" and that she was only looking for a book to read. She would have asked, but neither of you were here."

"And she just decided to look for one when Callie was outside, too."

"Why does that make you so suspicious?" Tim asked, rubbing the bridge of his nose to relieve some of the pressure he was feeling.

"She walked out without a book, she only went in there when she knew all of us, including Callie, were not in the house. You don't find that just a little suspect?"

"No, I really don't, Scott. I think that you and Emma want her out of here, so fine, I'll find a hotel for her. But I won't let her spend this time alone so don't expect me to be around for the holidays either."

"You're blackmailing me, seriously?"

Tim shrugged his shoulders. "I don't see what you see in her. There is a lot you don't know, Annie's had a significant amount of abuse in her life and she's fragile. She needs someone right now and I intend to be that someone, whether you like it or not."

"Damn, you really do care about her," Scott said quietly, running his fingers through his hair.

He hadn't even thought about what Annie might have been through in her life to make her the way that she was, and maybe he was being too judgy, but there were still many more questions about her than there were answers.

"Yes, I do, and I'm starting to get pretty irritated by your attitude."

Brown eyes met brown eyes and neither would look away. Scott wanted to reach over and shake some sense into his brother, but knew even that wouldn't work right now, Tim was too embroiled in his emotions. The more Scott fought him, the more he would bend over backwards in the opposite direction.

It took every ounce of his control, but Scott broke eye contact and blew out a long breath. "I'll give you the benefit of the doubt as far as she is concerned, but she's gone after Christmas, got it?"

"I understand," Tim said, standing up and walking back into the Great Room where the kids had almost finished decorating the tree.

"Hey, wait, I almost forgot something," Gabriel said, looking around in a panic.

"Right here," Hannah said with a smile, handing a small paper bag to him.

"What would I do without you?" he asked, his face splitting into an excited smile as he cautiously opened the bag and reached inside it.

"My mom sent this for you guys, for your tree. It's kind of a tradition in our family and she wanted to share it with you," Gabriel said. "Please, open it up and I'll explain."

Emma gingerly opened the brightly colored little box and pulled out a green glass Christmas ornament in the shape of a pickle. Emma had a quizzical look on her face as she held it up for everyone to see.

"We're German," Gabriel explained, as if that was all they needed to know.

"And?" Scott asked impatiently.

"You don't know the tradition of the Christmas Pickle?" Gabriel looked at Scott with pity, since he'd obviously missed out on something very important in his childhood.

Scott shook his head and so Gabriel enlightened him, and all the others.

"The Christmas pickle has to be the last ornament hidden on the tree. On Christmas morning, the child who finds it first receives an extra gift."

He pulled another little box out from behind his back. "Because you wouldn't have known to get an extra gift, my mom also sent this for whoever finds it on Christmas morning."

"What a wonderful woman, she is. I feel bad that we didn't invite her to be with us," Emma said, hugging Gabriel and then Hannah. "We'll be sure to do that next year."

"She would like that, thank you," Gabriel said, tearing up unexpectedly, trying to wipe his eyes quickly, before any of them could escape down his freckled cheek.

"But, Gabriel, aren't you an only child?" Scott asked.

"Yeah, why?"

"Is it safe to assume then, that you found the pickle every year?"

"Yes, it is," Gabriel responded proudly, and Scott just shook his head and took another swig of his beer before heading for one of the recliners.

His moment of relaxation was short-lived when the three kids nominated him to put the rainbow angel at the top of the tree.

"What the hell is a rainbow angel?" Scott asked Emma quietly.

"It's the tree topper, just a pretty angel who lights up all different colors."

After a bit of a struggle, Scott finally managed to get it to stand upright on the tree. The lights all worked, and with a big round of applause, the family celebrated their first Christmas tree in their new home.

"There's still plenty of afternoon left," Scott said. "How about we head into town, check out the sights, and you all let Emma and me take you out to dinner. We want to thank you for all the help we've had in so many different ways this year, the wedding, the house, and everything in between."

"Tim," Scott said, extending an olive branch, "do you want to see if Annie would be interested in joining us?"

"Yes, thanks." Tim seemed honestly grateful for the offer and hoped they might manage to get through the next few days pleasantly, after all.

Once they'd made their way into town, the small group wandered around for a little while, making their way towards the huge Christmas tree in the town park.

"Hey, Collin, you need to go over and sit on Santa's lap?" Scott asked, as Emma and Hannah stood in line, hoping to get a picture of Brian with Santa on his first Christmas, although you could barely even see the kid because he was so bundled up in a heavy snowsuit.

Collin looked at Scott sharply, bringing to mind the way his father had looked at Scott when they'd first met.

"I'm sixteen years old, I don't sit on Santa's lap." He hadn't spent a lot of time with Scott and still wasn't sure when he was joking and when he was serious.

"Sixteen, huh?"

"Yes."

"You driving yet?"

"A little bit. I have my permit but it's hard in the city, and my dad's pretty busy most of the time."

"Well, as long as the weather is cooperative, maybe I can take you out a few times while you're here."

"Really, in your Camaro? That would be so dope."

"What about me?" James asked.

"You aren't even close to old enough, are you?"

"I will be in a little over a year."

"Well then, remind me next year and we'll see what we can do."

Emma walked back to the little group a few minutes later with a happy smile on her face. They checked out the band playing Christmas carols in the large gazebo on the other side of the park and then the skating rink.

"That looks like fun," Shelly said, but her face didn't reflect her words.

"Why so sad then?" Tim asked.

"No skates. I outgrew mine years ago and never really had the opportunity since then, so I never got another pair."

Emma and Scott overheard her and their eyes met in a conspiratorial way. Skates and cross-country skis would be under the tree on Christmas morning for each of the three older kids, as well as Gabriel and Hannah, and Emma was getting even more excited about the upcoming holiday and the fun they were all going to have together while the kids were staying with them.

The temperature started dropping as the sun began to sink in the crisp, clear sky, so they decided to make their way to the restaurant.

They hadn't even managed to get out of the park yet when a large, burly man that was wearing a wool hunting coat, shoved his way through their little group.

The man walked straight into James, who took a header into the snow on the side of the path. James' face was flushed in embarrassment when he jumped back up to his feet.

"Hey, asshole," Scott said, taking several steps towards the man.

The behemoth turned and stared at Scott, then his eyes traveled around the rest of the group, pausing when he saw Annie snuggled up close to Tim's side.

"What the hell, buddy? There was no need for that, and I think an apology is in order."

The man's amber colored eyes slid back to meet Scott's, then he turned his head slightly and watched James viciously brushing the snow off his clothing.

"Stay out of my way next time," he said, his voice was a low, deep rumble. He met Annie's gaze one more time, then turned and walked away.

"Don't you walk away from me," Scott said, as he began to follow the man, but Emma grabbed his arm, holding him back.

"Let it go, Scott. James is fine and we are supposed to be enjoying ourselves."

"I would enjoy kicking his ass, doesn't that count?"

"Not today, it doesn't," she replied. "Come on, let's go."

Scott swallowed his anger and frustration and led the small group along the crowded sidewalk, elbow to elbow with the other harried shoppers. None of whom had an inkling of the virus that was starting to spread half a world away, and which would dramatically change all of their lives in just a few short months.

And, so they continued on, bumping into others and trying to avoid oversized shopping bags as they headed for the Italian restaurant just down the block.

It was an expensive restaurant and was filled with holiday revelers. They were given a large table in the backroom and, after they all got situated, Scott excused himself and made his way out to the main dining room.

He saw an older woman who was a member of the wait staff and who looked like she had quite a bit of experience with this restaurant. He made his way over to her and touched her arm to get her attention.

She was very busy and didn't appreciate the interruption but tried to remain polite.

"Have a seat, sir. Your waiter will be able to help you with whatever you need."

The information that Scott was after had to be obtained without anyone else hearing, but he couldn't tell her that.

"I'm sorry to bother you, but I have one quick question."

"What is it?"

"Is the silverware here real silver or is it stainless steel?"

"Why do you need to know that?" She looked at him in confusion.

"I just do. This is a pretty fancy restaurant, looks like real china and the cutlery looks like real silver. Is it? Simple question, I just need an honest answer."

The woman glanced the crowded room and then lifted her gaze to meet Scott's. "Of course, it's real silver, we wouldn't use anything but the best here."

"Excellent, thank you," he said, before making his way back to their table.

"Is everything alright?" Emma asked, when he returned.

Scott smiled and nodded. Dinner would cost him a pretty penny at this particular restaurant but would be worth every cent to finally confirm whether or not Annie was actually a shifter.

He tried not to stare in her direction as the waitress took their orders and then eventually returned with their starters. Emma followed his gaze and the two of them watched as Annie picked up her fork and started stabbing at her salad.

Scott turned to Emma and his face relaxed somewhat as he leaned over and whispered in her ear. "It's silver, she's okay. No need to worry about that, anymore."

Now that Emma's kids were there, Tim decided he would return home and let them all have a room of their own. He thought Annie would be alright by herself at this point and planned on heading back over the following day.

When he and his mom got back home, he decided to spend some time in the library and see if he could dig up any other info on shifters. They knew a lot about them, but apparently not enough.

"Good night, dear," Doris said, as she headed upstairs with Tolstoy on her heels. She stopped before she was even half-way up the steps and looked back over at Tim.

"It feels so nice having a big family now, doesn't it? And the kids, you and your brother weren't kids nearly long enough for me to enjoy, so having them around at the holidays feels very special. Life has been good to us since Emma became a part of ours, don't you think?"

"Yes, it has," Tim agreed. "It's certainly different than the quiet holidays that us three are used to."

"Definitely," she replied. "Good night, son."

Tim silently watched her walk up the stairs and pondered on how much things really had changed, and was pleased that the changes were affecting his mother in such a good way.

Somewhere in the back of his mind a small seed of hope was growing that one day his wife and kids would be a part of their lives, too, and his mother would be as happy and excited then, as she was now.

Shaking those thoughts from his head, trying not to dwell on what might never be, he wandered into the library and looked around in some of the ancient tomes, trying to determine which, if any, of them might hold the secrets to the shapeshifters that he needed.

Tim had barely settled down to start going through the first one when his phone buzzed.

"Hey, Rufus, what's up?"

"More bad news, my friend."

"What do you mean?"

"This damn creature is smarter than I gave him credit for, he's always a step ahead of me and its pissing me off."

"What happened?"

"I finally managed to locate the firm for that apartment building."

"That's good, right?"

"Would be, if I hadn't found the manager deader than a doornail inside it. And all the paperwork had been rifled through, a lot of it was destroyed and nothing was there about any Jason Turnbull. In fact, there was no paperwork for anyone in that apartment building at all, which leads me to believe it was the shifter covering his tracks. That thing does not want to be found."

"That sucks. I'm actually shocked that it had the wherewithal to know you would even go that route."

"Yeah, you and I were the only ones that knew I was checking into it, right?"

"I told Scott," Tim replied. "But I doubt he'd help out the shifter like that."

Rufus let loose a phlegmy cough as he started laughing. "Yeah, I tend to agree with you on that one. Well, keep your nose in the air, let me know if you hear about any deaths we might be able to blame on this guy and, like we talked about, I'll just have to follow the bodies."

"I'll do that. Stay safe, Rufus."

"You, too."

Tim leaned back in the oversized leather chair and picked up his snifter of brandy, a perfect nightcap for this particular day. But his face was tense and the lines across his forehead were deep as he considered this new bit of information.

He hadn't been completely honest with Rufus because Scott wasn't the only one that he'd told. Annie was there and she knew what their plan was, as well.

As suspicious as Scott and his mom were about her, Tim did not get the same vibe. In fact, his thoughts tended to go in the opposite direction.

He could feel her fear and trauma when they were together and couldn't believe that she would be able to fool him to that extent and so, he had faith in her that he might not have in someone else under the same circumstances.

That faith, however, was seriously challenged when he started flipping through the recent calls on his phone, although there was no particular reason for him to so.

He hesitated when he saw a New York number appear for a call that went out about a week before. He was not familiar with the number and was curious, so he called it.

After just a couple of rings, a man answered. "Annie, what's the matter, why are you calling on this phone?"

The man's voice was deep, it rumbled over the line and immediately brought to Tim's mind the large man that had knocked James into the snowbank earlier today.

"Who is this?" Tim asked. There was a moment of silence and then the line went dead. Tim knew there was no reason to call it again, it wouldn't be picked up again.

He leaned back, sipped his brandy and tried to deal with all the suspicious scenarios that were beginning to fill his head.

CHAPTER 13

"It was a lovely day, today, Scott, thank you." Brian was safely tucked away in his cradle and they were leaning back against the headrest of their bed. Scott had his arm wrapped protectively around Emma, pulling her up close against his side.

"Don't thank me, I didn't do anything."

"Stop it, you know that you did," she replied, lifting her brilliant green eyes to meet his. "You know how important this is to me. After all, it's our first holiday as a family and you started it out perfectly."

He kissed her lips gently, wondering how long it would be before they could do a whole lot more than that, but now was not the time to ask.

"I want it to be special, almost as much as you do. What's that?"

"It's Smoky, she's just prowling around."

"She going to stay in our part over here for the whole time?"

"It's probably for the best. From what Shelly told me, the cat got even more agitated about Annie than Callie did."

"She did. I don't want to worry you, but I do not trust that woman. I never hang my hat on any one thing, ever, but the reactions to her from the animals are very bothersome to me. I have to go with my gut and it's telling me that she's not what she seems."

"I agree," Emma said, and he could feel her shudder and tightened his grip on her.

"I have to figure out what to do. Tim spends a lot of time alone with her and I do trust his judgment, usually, but I can't understand why he is so dismissive about these strange things that keep popping up where she's concerned."

"I can't figure that one out, either. But I do know that, although she doesn't always seem to have normal reactions or emotions, she genuinely cares about Tim. I can see that in her eyes and on her face every time that he walks into the same room with her."

Scott shook his head. "I'm stumped. We finally know that she isn't a shifter, herself, but that doesn't mean there is nothing wrong with her. And we still don't know her true feelings for the shifter."

"You're still thinking about Stockholm syndrome?"

"It is possible, but I have no way of being able to verify that one way or another. At least not until it's too late to do anything about it."

Emma snuggled up against him a little closer and tried not to take his last comment to heart.

Scott realized he probably could have phrased that a little better and kissed the top of her head. "That particular scenario is unlikely, so don't get upset. It's entirely possible that she just has issues that we aren't privy to. Tim said Annie was abused when she was younger, maybe her coldness is just a result of that."

"Maybe," Emma said softly, "but it still doesn't explain Callie or Smoky and their reaction to her."

"No, it doesn't."

"Do you trust that silverware test?"

"I think we have to," Scott said. "Why?"

"I thought about asking her to leave but, that gets harder and harder to consider as we get closer to Christmas. If we're sure that she isn't an actual danger to us, then we might be over-reacting and turning her out alone for the holidays isn't really an option."

"I get what you're saying but, if things continue to get stranger or any more out of whack," Scott said, "it may very well come to that, Emma. You need to prepare yourself, just in case. The safety of our family has to take precedence over her spending Christmas alone, regardless of what her issues might be."

"I know. It's just that I truly do wish I could understand her better because I don't want that to have to happen."

"Me neither, and you should know that Tim already made it clear that if we kick her out, he'll go with her and won't be a part of our Christmas this year."

"Really? I can't believe he would choose Annie over his own mother. Do you think his feelings are deeper than we're giving him credit for?"

"Yup," Scott replied absently, twirling a strand of Emma's golden hair around his fingers, trying to swallow his annoyance at his brother for being so close-minded. "But it's his choice and he'll have to live with whatever he decides to do. It doesn't change our ability to make our own decisions about our home, our life and our family."

"Let's just hope we get through the next few days with no further drama. We'd better get to sleep now," she said, turning in his arms and kissing him lightly. "After all, we have a big day ahead of us tomorrow."

"What's tomorrow?"

"Cookie day, we'll be doing all kinds of baking. Your mom's coming over and Hannah, that girl is quite a baker by the way."

"What do I do?"

"You are so adorable. Maybe you should take Gabriel and the boys and go play in the snow."

"One day, in the not too distant future, we are going to have to have a real heart to heart conversation, son," Scott said, staring down into Brian's cherubic face.

The baby's eyes were wide and staring directly into his in such a way that Scott could almost believe he was hanging onto his every word.

They were alone in the baby's room and Scott was gently rocking him. He was beginning to feel more comfortable with the baby in his arms but still couldn't believe that he had played a part in creating this incredibly perfect child.

It was mind-blowing, and this was the first time he'd ever relaxed enough to actually have a conversation with Brian, albeit completely one-sided other than the occasional bubble escaping through Brian's lips.

"I'll have to explain about what I do for a living and tell you the truth about the monsters in your closet and the ones hiding under your bed. It's a conversation that I wish we would never have to have, but it isn't safe for you to live your life with your head stuck in the sand."

He smiled when Brian made some googly noises, as if he was trying to respond.

"I know, right?" Scott replied. "It's important that you know that I will always be here for you, your mom, and the rest of our family. You don't have to live your life in fear, but you will have to face reality and you must always be ready for the unexpected.

That's all I can do for you, prepare you for what might come. Hopefully, that won't have to happen until you are much older, when you can truly understand what's out there and the dangers that lurk in the dark. In the meantime, I'll always be here for you, never doubt that."

Scott stopped talking when he heard the sound of footsteps ringing out on the hardwood floors and then Shelly calling for her cat.

"Hey, Shelly," he called out. "Can you come in here for a minute?"

There was a hesitation in her response when she realized his voice was coming from the nursery. So far, she'd successfully avoided having anything to do with the baby, although whenever they were in the same room together, Shelly couldn't help but let her eyes glide over his way.

She wanted to take the little bundle into her arms, but she wasn't ready yet to embrace him as a part of her life and so she found it easier to just avoid being around him at all.

"I have to feed Smoky."

"Okay, but please stop in before you leave. I really could use your help."

He waited patiently as she found and fed her cat, dawdling as long she could by petting Smoky, dreading having to step into the nursery.

At long last, she did join him, although she barely stepped over the threshold. "What is it? I have to go help in the kitchen."

"Well, first," he said, "your mom told me that you think your friend, Madison, might not have too have long. I genuinely am sorry that we couldn't do more for her when all that shit went down over the summer. Are you doing okay with it?"

Shelly looked down at the light blue carpet under her feet and tears sprang into her eyes as she thought about losing one of her closest friends.

"Not so much. Some days, I don't think about it at all, then others, I can't get it out of my head."

Scott pursed his lips and wished he could make all of that go away for her, but it was a battle she would have to fight on her own.

"I'm here if you ever want to talk about it. I know it isn't something you can share with very many people, but don't ever think you can't come to me, alright?"

"Thank you," she said, blowing out a deep breath and blinking back her tears. "I may very well do that, but for the holidays, I promised myself that I wouldn't think about what happened or about losing Madison. There will be plenty of time in the future to dwell on it."

"Good for you," Scott said quietly. "I'm proud of you, so is your mom."

"Stop it," Shelly said, as the tears began to collect once again in her brilliant blue eyes.

"Sorry, I'm done talking about all that, but I do have another question for you."

She looked at Scott suspiciously as he awkwardly stood up from the rocking chair. "What?"

"Can you help me out with Brian?"

Scott knew the fact that Shelly wouldn't even acknowledge her baby brother was really eating at Emma and decided that it was a problem he should be able to rectify. He couldn't imagine that a better opportunity would present itself, so now was the time.

"What do you need?" she asked hesitantly.

"Am I even holding him right?"

Shelly took a step over closer. "You just have to be sure that his head is supported."

"Like this?" Scott asked, and Shelly started to giggle.

"What's so funny?"

"Well, it's just that your hands are almost bigger than he is."

"Here, you take him for a minute."

"I don't," she began, but was too late, Scott was holding the little bundle out to her and Shelly had no choice but to grab onto it and adjust Brian safely in her arms.

He was awake, making motions with his lips like a fish and his wide eyes were staring straight into hers, as if he knew she was a conquest that he needed to make, and her heart melted immediately.

"He's so freaking cute," she said quietly, sitting down on the rocking chair and moving back and forth with him, their eyes still locked.

"Let me know if you need anything," Scott said quietly, making his way over towards the door, but Shelly didn't respond because her complete attention was now focused on her baby brother.

Doris had arrived with Tolstoy and walked into the house with Hannah and Gabriel while Scott was in the baby's room with Shelly.

When he walked into the kitchen and found everyone congregating there, Scott began to feel a little claustrophobic. He was happy to have everyone in their home, but he'd spent the majority of his life with only one or two people around him most of the time and this crowd was beginning to make him feel a little caged in and overwhelmed.

"Gabriel, James and Collin," he called out sharply, and the various voices in the room quieted as all heads turned in his direction.

"Boots, gloves, coats, let's go. Gabriel and I made paths for the snowmobiles and there's even a few jumps, if you're men enough to try them."

He winked at Emma when he saw the expression of horror on her face.

Gabriel's things were right there in the kitchen and the two boys ran upstairs to get the rest of their gear.

"Mom," Scott asked, stepping closer to her and putting his arm around her shoulder, "are you making your gingerbread whoopie pies? You know they're my favorite, right?"

She grabbed the beard hairs on his chin and yanked them playfully. "Oh course, I'm making them. I can't have you crying like a spoiled baby on Christmas, can I?"

"Which reminds me," Emma said, "where's Brian? I thought you had him."

"Right here," Shelly replied, as she came in to join the others, rocking her brother in her arms. "He's almost asleep, I'll just hold him for now if that's alright."

"Certainly," Emma said, and Scott was gratified to see the happiness making her face positively glow as she watched her daughter finally bonding with her new brother.

Emma's eyes slid over to Scott's and she mouthed the words, 'thank you'.

He gave her an exaggerated wink, then turned to his own mother. "Hey, Mom, is Tim coming over?"

"Yes, he was finishing up something and said he'd head out after that."

"Well, let him know where we are, he's welcome to come join us if he wants."

"I'll do that, but can you do me a favor, Scott?" Doris asked, eying Tolstoy, who was relentlessly teasing Callie over on her bed in the corner of the kitchen. "Would you mind taking Tolstoy with you? It'll be good exercise for him, and it'll get him out from underneath our feet for a little while."

"Sure," he replied, throwing on his own coat and boots and calling to the dog as he walked out the door with Gabriel. "Send the boys out to the barn when they're ready."

Once the women were left to their own devices in the kitchen there was a collective sigh of relief and then they rolled up their sleeves and got to work.

They sat together at the island, pouring over their recipes and determining which items would need to be done first. They'd made good progress and were starting to put together the ingredients for their various assigned goodies when Tim showed up.

"They all went snowmobiling," Doris said. "You can go join them if you'd like."

Tim looked around the bustling room, there were all manner of dry ingredients, eggs, milk, and numerous spices lined up on one of the counters. He certainly had no desire to hang out in the kitchen, but he also knew there were only four snowmobiles and he thought he'd let Scott have a chance to spend time with Emma's boys.

Besides, he needed to have a private chat with Annie about some things and this appeared to be a perfect opportunity to do that.

"I think I'll go see if Annie would like to take a walk. It's beautiful outside, crisp, but not brutal cold."

"Enjoy yourself," Doris replied absently, as she started assembling the ingredients for her whoopie pies.

Hannah was already busy making her own specialty, Peppermint Bark cannolis, and Emma started working on the obligatory sugar cookies.

Callie growled once and they all turned to look over at her in the corner. She stayed on her bed, but Emma could see the hair on the nape of her neck rising as Tim and Annie walked in. Annie eyed her suspiciously and Emma made her way over to Callie's side, to pet and reassure her until the two of them made their way outside through the back door.

Once they did, she walked over to the sink to scrub her hands and felt the need to unload before returning to her cookie batter.

"I truly cannot understand Callie's reaction to that woman. She's never behaved that way before towards anyone."

"It is strange," Doris said.

"How is she with Tolstoy?" Emma asked.

Doris hesitated, lifting the wooden spoon out of the large bowl where she was mixing the ingredients for her whoopie pies, and then replied, "I believe they've only been together the one time at my house, and he did get wonky. I had to put him in his crate in another room. Tolstoy didn't act like he wanted to attack her, he just wouldn't stop barking. It was bizarre."

"Has he been around her at all when you've been here?"

"Let me think, the day we did the tree, Tim asked me to keep him home. As far as I can recall, any other time that I've had him here, either the dog is outside when Annie's downstairs or she's upstairs when he's in the house. Like I said, it's quite strange."

"Do you think that Tim really likes Annie?" Hannah asked shyly.

"I'm afraid that he does," Doris replied.

"Is that a bad thing?"

"Not really," Doris replied. "I know I should be less judgy, but he is my baby boy, after all."

Emma met her eyes and they smiled because she'd felt the same about Emma in the beginning.

"Didn't I hear that Tim was engaged once upon a time?" Emma asked.

"He was," Doris said, pursing her lips as she let her mind wander back to that time. "A lovely girl, local, her name is Sarah. I still see her from time to time in town."

"What happened?" Hannah asked. "Why didn't they get married?"

"I don't know," Doris replied. "And it makes me crazy. My boys tell me almost everything, but that is the one taboo subject between Tim and me. I don't even think Scott knows the reason why."

"Oh, I'll have to try and find out," Emma said. "I love a mystery."

"Whatever you do, don't bring it up to Tim. I think she was the one true love of his life and he hasn't ever gotten over her."

"How sad," Hannah said, feeling so grateful to have found Gabriel.

"Couldn't we try and fix the two of them up?" Shelly asked. She was sitting comfortably over at the table, trying to keep her voice low so that she wouldn't wake Brian.

"I've considered that, especially lately, but," Doris said, "if he really does like this Annie girl, the timing just isn't good. I wouldn't want him to think I was only doing it to keep him away from Annie. All that would do is push him even further along in her direction."

CHAPTER 14

Unaware that he was currently the topic of the women's conversation, Tim walked slowly down the trail into the woods, holding Annie's hand in his own, which was a bit difficult because of the bulky gloves they were wearing.

"Did you enjoy yourself yesterday?" he asked.

"It was fine. I do feel like kind of an outsider, I'm not a member of your family and probably shouldn't have gone."

"I wanted you to go. I wanted you to spend the day with me and my family."

"You really are sweet," she replied, "but I keep thinking about the upcoming holidays and that maybe I shouldn't stay. It should be for just your family."

"You're missing my point," Tim said. "It's my holiday, as well, and you'll ruin it for me if you aren't a part of it."

She slid her eyes toward his and Tim could see the doubt that remained in them and decided to try a different tack.

"Christmas is only a few days away. I don't want you out there all by yourself, not when Jason is still free."

"What's going on with that, anyway? Any idea where he is?"

"No, Rufus found the company that owns the apartment building, but the manager was dead. Looks like Jason killed him and destroyed any paper trail that might have led us to him."

"That's horrible," she said softly.

Tim was still watching Annie's face as they walked, and her expression never changed. The cool breeze was turning her cheeks pink, but there was no fear on her face, no disgust at the thought that Jason had killed another person, and he started to feel a sharp pain jabbing in his chest.

Annie's physical reaction, once again, didn't seem to match her verbal response. It was as if she had the intellect to know the proper words to say but wasn't able to muster the appropriate emotion to match those words.

Not for the first time, Tim couldn't help but wonder if he might be completely wrong about her, after all.

"I have to ask you a question and please don't be offended."

She stopped walking and turned towards him, her hazel eyes sometimes looked more green or gold than brown and, today, with the brilliant snow reflecting in them, he couldn't miss the golden shards staring back at him suspiciously.

"When you borrowed my phone in the beginning, who did you call?"

"Why do you ask?"

"Because I want to know who you called."

She didn't answer right away. Annie always seemed to hold her cards close to her vest and Tim's stomach roiled as he realized she may well just be giving herself enough time to come up with a believable lie.

"Was that the first day I was here?"

"Yes, you didn't have the charger for your own phone and had to borrow mine."

"I remember now," she said, looking down into the snow. "I had to call my boss and let him know that I wouldn't be coming in to work for awhile."

"Did you call your office?"

"This sounds a bit like an interrogation, Tim. What's going on?"

"Just please answer that question, did you call the office?"

"No, I have my boss' personal cell number and that's what I called. I wanted to actually speak with him, not just leave some kind of weird message. Now you answer my question, why do you want to know?"

"I saw the strange number on my phone last night and called it. The man that answered hung up on me and wouldn't tell me who he was, seemed a little odd."

"You were checking up on me?" she asked, and her eyes narrowed even more.

"No, I didn't even remember that you used the phone until afterwards. I was just curious about the strange number that I saw on it."

"Do you want me to leave?"

"Of course not, we just went over that."

"It's obvious that you, and your brother, have some suspicions about me. What I cannot understand is why. I didn't come to you, you came to me and all but forced me to leave my own home and come here. So, what is your issue? What do you think that I'm trying to do that is so terrible?"

Tears suddenly filled her eyes and Tim remembered what she'd said about her past. He pulled off a glove and wiped the tear away that was sliding down her cheek.

"I'm sorry," he said, but she kept her eyes down and wouldn't meet his.

"You didn't answer me," she said quietly.

"Nothing, we don't suspect you of anything, please believe me," he added, when she finally did raise her eyes and he could see the doubt that remained in them.

"What is all this about then?"

Her point was valid, and she certainly had a way of turning his thoughts completely topsy-turvy from one minute to the next. He was used to trusting his own instincts but, right now, he wasn't sure what was real and what wasn't as far she was concerned.

He felt like he was constantly flip-flopping as far his feelings and beliefs about her. It was draining and exhausting and he was tired of these niggling doubts eating away at him.

They slowly started walking down the trail again. The cold wind was bracing, but it helped Tim focus and get his thoughts together before replying.

"I don't know the answer to your question other than the fact that you are different from anyone that I've ever met. To be honest, I do have a very suspicious nature and I question everything. You can't take it personal, it's a part of who I am."

"How can I not take it personal when you're interrogating me and judging me for something that I'm not even aware that I've done? It seems that whenever you and I might be making a real connection, suddenly your suspicions rear their ugly head and you drive a wedge between us. Why is that?"

"I guess I have been doing that, haven't I?" he replied, sighing heavily. "I can't answer your question with any certainty, other than to tell you that I haven't had much luck in my love life either. Sometimes, I think that I might be trying to sabotage myself to make sure that I always end up alone. Maybe that's what I'm doing with you. I really don't know."

They continued trudging silently through the snow for a few minutes.

"So," Annie finally said, "we're just two misfits and we're having a little trouble navigating this particular path that we're on, is that it?"

"I think maybe it is."

"And how do we rectify that situation?"

"Maybe this little talk was a step in the right direction," he said, turning towards her and pushing her hood back, running his fingers through her thick curly hair as he lowered his lips towards hers. And this time, the passion in her response as she melted against him, left him with no doubt that her emotions matched the deed.

"What was that?" he said, pulling back and looking into the trees around them.

"I didn't hear anything," she replied.

"A large branch snapped, and it was close."

"The dog from the other day?" she asked, her panic rising.

"No, I doubt that," he said, still trying to peer into the dense evergreens.

"Let's go back, I don't want to be out here anymore."

Tim looked around one more time, then they turned and made their way towards the house, although the hair rose on the back of his neck and he was sure that someone, or something, was still watching them.

A low growl emanated from the creature's chest as he watched Tim and Annie head down the path. His entire being was filled with fury. If he didn't know better, he'd think that his Annie was starting to have feelings for the hunter, and that was not acceptable.

He paced in a tight circle amongst the thick copse of evergreen trees. He'd been staying back in the trees, out of sight of the humans on their noisy snowmobiles, yet close enough to keep an eye on what they were doing while he tried to come up with a game plan.

The arrival of Tim and Annie had been an unexpected and unwelcome sight and he was extremely agitated now.

He heard one of the snowmobiles splutter into silence, not far from where he was, then he heard a young man's voice uttering some descriptive swear words and started to make his way stealthily through the trees, heading in that direction.

"What the hell?" James exclaimed, as the engine spluttered into silence, leaving him back far behind the others.

"How come I got this stupid, piece of shit sled?" He yelled out to no one in particular. It was the second time it had just quit and was very frustrating.

"Screw it," he said, taking advantage of the downtime to step off the trail and relieve himself before trying to start the damn thing again.

He wouldn't have dallied, however, had he known that the creature was silently making its way towards him. It stopped and watched the boy for a moment to ascertain the threat level. Determining that it was minimal, he stealthily crept closer.

James walked back over to his sled and tried the starter again. At first there was nothing, but then the engine sounded like it wanted to catch, and he took heart that he may not have to walk all the way back to the house, after all.

The creature moved in on him and was now close enough that one long bound would put him on top of the boy; a quick bite to the neck and it would be over in seconds. The creature could feel the spread of adrenaline surge through its body at the thought of the impending attack.

But, just as he bunched his muscles in preparation of launching his body forward onto the boy, something that had been moving through the snow as silently as he had attacked from the rear.

He felt long canine teeth bury themselves into his shoulder, barely missing the soft tissue of his neck, which may very well have been fatal. With a sinister growl he turned to do battle with his attacker.

James thought he heard something in the trees behind him, but just then the engine caught with a loud rumble and he breathed a sigh of relief and headed off down the trail towards the others.

Tolstoy was still a young dog that had no fighting experience, but with every fiber of his being, he knew this creature was a danger to his family and must be destroyed. With teeth exposed and growling from deep down in their chests, the two attacked head on, trying to wound their opponent while protecting their own most vulnerable areas.

Tolstoy gave his all, but the creature was larger and easily outmaneuvered the pup. It bit him hard on the shoulder and, as Tolstoy yelped and backed away, the creature swept out with its paw and dragged its long claws deeply into Tolstoy's side, watching as blood instantly turned the snow red beneath him.

Tolstoy's yelp changed to a whine, but he would not give up. He took a hesitant step forward towards the creature, ignoring the pain screaming through his body and the creature braced, ready to make its final, deadly attack.

But when the buzz of snowmobile engines suddenly drew closer, it hesitated. The creature was suffering from wounds of its own and, although it was not losing blood as fast as Tolstoy, the injuries were still significant.

It so badly wanted to finish off the dog, but couldn't take the chance because the sleds were getting closer every second. Besides, the dog was in bad straights and there was a good chance it might die, anyway. With one last horrific snarl in Tolstoy's direction, the creature sprinted into the woods.

Tolstoy watched the creature run off and then let out a mournful howl as he finally allowed himself to lay down in the bloody snow.

The women had made good headway in their baking endeavors by mid-day and cleared some counter space to put out items for lunch since the boys should be back at any time.

Tim and Annie had returned a little earlier and were now upstairs together.

The mood was light and other than the faint odor of burnt cookies, the mouth-watering smells from the other various baked goods wafted throughout the house. Only one batch had been a slightly overcooked, much to Emma's chagrin, but there was no time to dwell on it as she got the next set of cookie trays ready.

The smooth and steady workflow ended abruptly when they heard the snowmobiles approaching. Emma went over to peer out the back door since it sounded like at least one of them was coming this way, rather than returning to the barn.

Her eyes opened wide when she saw Gabriel riding on the back of Scott's sled, which slid to a stop on the back sidewalk.

"Oh, no," she said quietly, opening the door as the two of them hurried in. "What happened?"

"Not sure, looks like he ran into something bigger and meaner than he was," Scott replied, carrying Tolstoy in his arms.

The pup was about seven months old and easily weighed at least fifty pounds so that was not necessarily an easy task.

Doris hurried over, her hand on her chest as she tried to quiet her pounding heart.

"How bad is he?" she asked, trying to remain calm.

"He has some really deep cuts and bites and has lost quite a bit of blood. Let me take him into the breezeway so we can check him out closer without making a mess in here."

"There's a cabinet in there with some sheets and towels," Emma said. "What else will we need?"

"A large bowl or bucket of warm water," Doris replied, as she threw on her coat and ran out to her car to grab the emergency first aid kit which she had stashed in the trunk.

Emma grabbed the water and followed along after Scott. Gabriel was standing at the door, looking unsure of himself.

He met Hannah's worried eyes and forced a smile onto his face. "The rest of us are fine, we have to go back and get the other sled though. I'll grab one of the boys and we'll be back in just a few minutes."

"Is it safe out there?"

"Oh, sure," he replied, but he was not anywhere near as confident as he was pretending to be.

Doris was back by then and hurried past the others to get to her pup. He'd become her closest friend in the short time she'd had him, and she cared as much for him as if he were one her sons.

Tolstoy was whining when she approached, and her heart hurt for him as she gently ran her fingers along one side.

"Scott, can you turn him over for me?"

He did so, as gently as he could, and Doris got a better look at the worst of the damage. Gabriel had used his scarf to wrap the wounds and staunch the flow of blood, which had probably saved the dog's life.

"Do we need to get him to a vet?"

"I'm not sure," Doris replied. "If it was you or Tim, I could sew it up myself, but I'm not sure about Tolstoy. If I hurt him, he won't understand so he probably should be knocked out first. Those cuts are pretty deep and since we don't know what wounded him, he should probably get on anti-biotics, as well. You don't know what it was, do you?"

"No, I don't."

"I can drive you to the vet's office, Doris," Shelly offered, she'd walked up on them so quietly that no one heard her.

"Thank you, dear, that would be very helpful. My car is bigger so, Scott, can you carry him out for me?" Doris asked, as she wrapped one of the clean sheets securely around him.

Poor Tolstoy, who was normally full of boundless energy, was now laying quietly, panting and whining, and it broke Doris' heart.

"Sure," he replied, gently lifting the dog and carrying him out to the car.

"I'll call the animal hospital and let them know you're coming. Shelly, drive careful, alright?"

"I will."

Once Shelly and Doris headed out, the others congregated in the kitchen.

"Man, it smells good in here," Scott said, but he was distracted by what had happened to Tolstoy.

Emma walked over to Hannah to relieve her of the baby that Shelly had foisted upon her before going into the breezeway.

Scott looked around and saw that James had made his way back into the house. "Where are Gabriel and Collin?"

"They went back to get the other sled that we left in the woods."

"Damn it," Scott said, "they should have waited."

"What's going on, Scott, really?" Emma asked.

Ignoring the question, he asked one of his own. "Tim's here, isn't he?"

"Yes, he's upstairs with Annie."

"Let me go get him and then I'll explain to everyone at the same time."

He bellowed up the stairs and within a few moments Tim and Annie appeared. Callie let out a soft growl but stayed in her corner and Annie made sure to stand back behind Tim while she kept a wary eye on the dog.

Tim saw that Emma was cleaning up spots of blood on the floor and knew something bad had happened.

"What's up?"

Scott ran his fingers roughly through his hair. "Tolstoy came with us this morning. We spent a lot of time in that one clearing where we'd built the jumps and he was with us almost the whole time. I didn't notice he took off until we decided to head back and assumed he'd already returned to the house on his own."

He paused and ran his fingers through his hair again. "Halfway back, we saw him lying just off to the side of the trail in a patch bloody snow. I was afraid he was dead but he's still kicking. Mom and Shelly just took him to the vet."

"What happened to him?" Tim asked.

"Some kind of animal," Scott said. "He had some deep claw marks on his side and he'd been bitten a few times, as well. He has blood around his muzzle, but I don't think it's his own, I think he put up a hell of a fight and that's why he's still alive."

"What do you want to do?" Tim asked.

"A little hunting, you want to come with?"

"Sounds good. I'll go get the rifle out of my truck."

"I'll get my stuff and meet you at the barn."

A few minutes later they were both gone and Emma looked around, trying to wrap her head around all of this new drama. She was worried about Tolstoy, about Gabriel and Collin, and now she could add Scott and Tim to that list.

"Hannah, I'm going to go lay Brian down and I'll be right back."

Poor Hannah looked frightened to death as she wrung her hands together and stared out the window, waiting for Gabriel to return.

Emma returned to the kitchen a few minutes later and grabbed the bread, sandwich meat and chips and laid them out on the large island in the center of the room right next to the paper plates.

"Grab something to eat, Hannah. The others will be back shortly." Then she looked around in confusion.

"I thought Annie came down with Tim."

"She did but, I think she went back upstairs when he left with Scott."

Emma went to the bottom of the stairs and called up to her, "Annie, do you want some lunch?"

There was no response. "Annie, if you would like something to eat, please come down and help yourself."

She had neither the time, nor the energy, to deal with any of Annie's drama today so, when there was no response that time either, Emma headed back out and grabbed something to eat for herself, as did James and Hannah, although none of them felt all that hungry just now.

CHAPTER 15

Scott and Tim met up in the barn and Scott filled two of the sleds with gas.

"We can take these to where we found Tolstoy. From there, we can pick up the tracks and, hopefully, kill the son of a bitch."

"What do you think it was?"

"How the hell do I know? You saw some tracks a week or so ago, right?"

"Yeah, and we went for a walk earlier today and I think there was something nearby in the woods."

"Today, and you didn't bother to try and find out what it was?"

"Something broke a branch, could have a been a deer, could have been anything. Annie got scared, she thought it might be a dog, so we headed back."

"You really have lost your edge and I think it's because of Annie. Seriously, how could you not check that out?"

"Excuse me all to hell, Scott. You have a problem with me, fine, but you leave Annie out of this, understand? Now, do you want my help or not?"

Scott glared at him, frustrated at brother's behavior and the fact that he refused to see that Annie was not at all what she seemed to be. She was playing him like a fiddle and he refused to even discuss the possibility that there might be a real problem with her.

Scott stopped before turning on the engine and looked over at his brother. "Do you think this is definitely an animal? Could it be the shifter?"

"Anything is possible," Tim replied, with a shrug of his shoulders, "but there's no way it should have been able to find us. For now, in my mind anyway, it's just an animal."

Scott wondered once again about Annie and how deep her ties were with the shifter but kept his thoughts to himself. Tim was not being realistic about this situation and it was frustrating for Scott to have to tiptoe around some obvious concerns when discussing them with his brother.

"Take that one," he said, then maneuvered his sled into position and headed out of the barn and down the trail. There was one adrenaline filled moment just after they headed out, when Scott rounded a corner going full-throttle and he and Gabriel almost collided head-on.

He was so intent on catching up to whatever it was that had attacked Tolstoy that he completely forgot that Gabriel and Collin still had to make their way back to the house on the same trail.

The two of them swerved at the last minute and Gabriel safely managed to continue on his way. Collin was a short distance behind him and by the time he had to pass, Scott and Tim had slowed their machines down to almost a standstill.

A few minutes later, the two brothers parked their sleds near the bloody snow where Tolstoy had fallen and found that Scott was correct. Tolstoy must have put up a good fight because not only did they have tracks to follow, but there were drops of blood leading off into the woods, as well, confirming the creature was also injured.

"What do you think?" Scott asked. "Big-ass dog, or a wolf?"

"I'm not sure and I guess it doesn't much matter does it? Looks like the blood trail is tapering off which is strange, if it's continuing to move, the blood would continue flowing. It wouldn't clot up in the wound unless it was bound or if it stopped moving for awhile."

"If it stopped, we shouldn't be all that far behind."

They continued on for another ten minutes or so, the snow was deep, but the creature had made a bit of a path through it already, allowing them to move fairly quickly. The tracks in the fresh snow were easy to see and Scott and Tim were confident they were heading in the right direction. The animal couldn't have been injured too badly, though, if it was able to make it this far.

"Son of a bitch," Scott said a short time later, stopping abruptly.

"What's wrong?" Tim asked.

"It crossed the road."

The two men checked out the road itself, which was covered with slush and salt, but enough time had passed that traffic had annihilated any trace of its pawprints and they had no idea what direction it would have gone. The only thing they could see on the road itself, was one lonely car, way off in the distance, almost out of sight.

Scott jogged over to the other side of the road and turned towards Tim, shaking his head.

"No tracks over here, it must have headed down the road."

"Clever little bastard, isn't it?" Tim said. "Guess we can turn back. I can't figure where it would be heading though. In either direction, it's bound to run into populated areas. Why wouldn't it cross the road and stay hidden in the woods where it would be safer?"

"I think it's acting just a little too clever," Scott replied.

"What do you mean?"

Scott ran his fingers roughly through his thick hair and frowned. "Think about it, Tim. This thing, whatever it is, knew enough to stanch the blood flow from its wounds and to hit the highway so we couldn't track it any farther. An animal doesn't know enough to do that."

"You're back to it being the shifter?" Tim asked, exhaling a deep breath and rolling his eyes.

"Why are you so sure it can't be the creature?"

"There is no way it would be been able to find us. I never had any direct contact with it, and it would have no way of knowing that Annie is here with us. It isn't possible."

"Can you give me the benefit of the doubt, just this once?" Scott asked, ignoring his brother's raised eyebrow. "I'm not saying it's the creature for sure, but the possibility does exist and we need to be prepared. Just in case. Can you at least agree with that?"

"Fine, I'll keep my eye out for anything odd. Are we done?"

He knew Scott well enough to be able to read between the lines and know that, in Scott's mind, Annie may well have sold them all out to the shifter. But that made no sense because she was scared to death at the thought of the shifter and certainly wouldn't have given it her location.

Scott shook his head in frustration as the two of them turned and headed back through the woods. They made it back to the house by mid-afternoon, both of them cold, hungry and more than a little cranky.

Taking off his coat and boots, Scott turned and got a good look at Gabriel.

"What the hell happened to you?"

Gabriel self-consciously raised his hand to his cheek and covered the welts.

"Dang cat's back in the barn and meaner than ever. Scared the crap out of me. I yelled, it hissed and took a swipe at me, then took off."

"What cat?" Tim asked.

"Gabriel found a black cat in the barn a week or so ago, but then it disappeared. Guess it's back again."

"And what did you two find?"

"A whole lot of tracks," Scott replied, turning towards the kitchen doorway when he heard Annie come down to join them. "They disappeared on the road so, whatever it was should be miles away by now, but everyone be careful when you go outside. No one goes alone and no one goes far from the house, understood?"

He looked at each of them, one by one, to make sure that they were listening. Something was going on and, although he couldn't put his finger on exactly what it was, he knew it held great danger for his family.

Scott didn't want to frighten Emma or the kids unnecessarily, but he needed to be sure they wouldn't wander far from the house.

"We can still go out on the snowmobiles, can't we?" Collin asked.

"Only if I go with you."

Collin pouted and kicked his foot back and forth against the hardwood floor, he wasn't a child anymore and didn't like to be treated like one.

"Any word from Mom?" Tim asked.

"Shelly called and the vet was able to stitch up Tolstoy. She's dropping them both off at Doris' house now."

Scott's nose lifted in the air and his stomach growled.

"Smells great in here, any of these cookies need taste testing?"

"Help yourself, we can always make more."

Jason was in a foul mood as he drove down the road, he'd managed to temporarily stop the bleeding from the deep wound in his shoulder, but there were others, shallower but which still needed to be dressed.

He was currently wearing Al Boyd, so he returned to his disgusting house to clean up his injuries. The pup was strong, and he was bruised as well as bloodied, but all of those injuries would heal on their own before too long.

After tending his wounds, Jason laid on the couch, staring at the ceiling, thinking about everything that had gone wrong; first it was seeing Annie and the hunter; then missing out on the boy; being caught by surprise by the young pup; actually suffering injuries in the fight and then being chased by the two hunters.

They hadn't been far behind him by the time he reached his car, which was hidden out of sight. Jason had hopped into it naked and took off, not willing to risk even those few moments that it would have taken to put on his clothes.

He worried for a minute that the car might be stuck in the new snow but, fortunately, he had four-wheel drive and plowed through the light fluff and onto the roadway.

He was far enough away that he was barely able to see the hunters in his rearview mirror when they walked out of the woods and onto the road.

His anger festered inside of him until he couldn't stand it any longer. This situation needed to be rectified, no more reconnaissance, it was time to start eliminating his foes. That was the only way he would be able to take Annie back and continue life with her by his side.

Jason knew the original hunter was still on his trail and decided he would take care of that one first, just to make sure he would no longer be any problem, whatsoever. After that, the two younger hunters and their family would be a piece of cake.

A smile spread on his face as he anticipated the bloody melodrama that would be unfolding over the next couple of days.

"Are you sure you don't mind, Tim?"

"Of course not, Mom, do you need anything else besides the peanut butter?"

"No, I've tried everything I have in the house to get him to take those stupid anti-biotic pills, even cheese, which he loves, but Tolstoy is just spitting out the pills and wolfing down the cheese.

I think peanut butter is the only answer and I don't want to leave him just now. He's still pretty sore and needy."

"You treat him just like a kid," Tim replied, with a shake of his head.

"What do you care? I do the same for you."

"Good point," he acknowledged. "You win. I'm out of here and I'll be back in a bit."

"Good morning, Rufus, what's up? Did you find the creature?" Tim asked, a few minutes later when the call came in as he was driving to the store.

"I think I might have."

"That's great, you need help finishing it off? I'm on my way into town right now, but I can head out shortly if you need me."

"Yes and no," Rufus replied.

"What do you mean?"

"Yes, I could use some help, but no, not great."

"What are you saying? Spit it out, Rufus."

It was not like Rufus to be so ambiguous and Tim was getting frustrated with him.

"I'm in Edgewater, Tim."

"My Edgewater?"

"Yes, I've been looking for similar kills and I finally found one, just the other side of Edgewater from where you and your family live."

"How did Scott and I miss it?"

"Hasn't hit the wire yet, I heard it on the scanner. It just happened, either over night or real early this morning."

"Damn, I'll have to let Scott know. Where are you right now?"

"Out where it happened, there's an old abandoned factory about ten miles outside the west side of town. The cops finally finished up and left a little bit ago."

"Mackenzie's?"

"Yeah, that's the place."

"I can be there in about twenty minutes. Wait for me, alright?"

"Sure," Rufus replied, before hanging up.

Tim called Scott but just got his voicemail. "Scott, it's Tim. Hey, I just heard from Rufus and we've got a problem. Call me as soon as you get this."

The roads weren't horribly bad, but some idiot had slid into a snowbank and was partially blocking the road just outside of town. Tim was finally able to maneuver past it along with the other cars in front of him, but it was closer to a half an hour before he arrived at the factory. He found Rufus' beat up pick truck in the parking lot and pulled in beside it.

"Hey, Rufus," he called, rapping on the driver side window, but there was no response.

The police, coroner, and whoever else had been at the scene of the crime, left the parking lot filled with tire tracks and footprints heading every which way.

It was currently empty except for Rufus' truck, so he had to assume that Rufus had headed into the building on his own. Tim shook his head in frustration and made his way over to the path leading to the entrance of the cavernous old building.

"Damn it, why didn't you wait?" Tim muttered, as he made his way inside.

There were windows all along the outer wall and the light filtering in was sufficient to see where he was going, he didn't know where the incident had happened but was able to follow the wet footprints down one long hallway filled with offices, which eventually led him to the warehouse.

The building smelled damp and unused and his footsteps echoed loudly in the emptiness.

About halfway down the hall, the water and slush on the floor became a blurry mess, as if someone had scuffed through it. Stepping around that area and continuing on, Tim noticed that at least one set of footprints were now taking on a reddish hue and he could see the spots of blood that had dripped alongside them.

The red became more prominent and then those footprints disappeared completely and were replaced by rusty colored drag marks in the slush along the hallway. Tim slowly reached for his pistol and turned off the safety, the cops wouldn't have walked back and forth through this so he could only assume it had happened since they left.

Tim tried to envision what had happened to explain what he was seeing. There must have been some sort of a scuffle, one of the parties was injured and was being forced along towards the warehouse. Unable to walk any further, it looked like the injured person then had to be dragged.

At the end of the hallway there was a set of swinging doors that led into the warehouse. One of the doors had been propped open so the police could come and go as needed. Tim sidled through and turned his whole body in a semi-circle with the gun held at the ready, as he searched for any movement.

Everything remained still and quiet.

"Rufus," he called out, ignoring the eerie echoing of his own voice. "Rufus, hey man, where are you?"

He slowly started following the bloody drag marks down between the tall, empty shelves, constantly on the alert for any noise or sign of movement, but none came.

At the end of one long section, he lowered his gun and ran over to Rufus' body which had been dragged around the corner.

He put his fingers to Rufus' carotid artery just to be sure, but it was obvious that he was already gone.

His entire chest had been torn out and what little blood was left had pooled on the floor underneath him.

"Damn it, Rufus. Why didn't you wait for me?" He shook his head and closed his friend's eyelids.

Rufus hadn't been dead for long, but with no other sounds or movement, Tim didn't think the shifter could still be in the building. Even so, he kept his guard up as he found something to wrap Rufus' body in and then carried it out to his truck, securing it in the bed, under the cap, until he and Scott could take care of it properly.

Tim knew this was not his fault, but he still felt guilty for not being there in time to help out his old friend. They'd had some good times together over the years and Rufus could always be counted on to be there when they needed him. It wasn't right that he had gone out this way.

Shaking himself out of his reverie, Tim jumped into the truck and headed out. He needed to get to Scott and Emma's as soon as possible. If the shifter was this close, he may already know where they lived and could be on his way there right now.

Tim did have to acknowledge that Scott's instincts about the creature in the woods being the shifter had been spot on and he should have respected them.

He thought about calling Scott again, but he'd already left one message and hadn't heard back yet, besides the initial conversation between them would have to be done in private, so he set the phone down on the passenger seat and headed out of the parking lot.

Tim was filled with an urgency that he couldn't explain and drove as fast as he safely could until he pulled up to their house. Unfortunately, as horrible as this day had already been, it was about to get much worse.

"Hey, Tim, come on in," Scott said, as he opened the front door. Tim's nose was filled with the balsam scent from the brightly decorated wreath hanging on it, but he paid no attention because of the next words that Scott uttered.

"We're all in the Good Room and we have unexpected company."

"Who?"

"You'll see," Scott replied, and Tim almost bit straight through his tongue when he saw Rufus sitting on the couch in between Emma and Shelly.

CHAPTER 16

Tim's eyes swept around the room, trying to gauge the extent of the threat. Emma's three kids were in there, as was Annie. Emma was holding the baby and Rufus was bent over it, oohing and awing as Tim entered the room.

"Holy shit," Tim said, then recovered as quickly as he could. "What the hell are you doing here, Rufus?"

"Missed you guys and thought I'd stop in with a little holiday cheer."

"The good stuff," Scott said, holding up a bottle of his favorite scotch.

"Actually, I was in the area on a job and thought I'd check in since I was so close."

If Tim didn't know that Rufus' dead body was outside in the back of his pickup, he would never have known this was the shifter. But he did know, and now he had to figure out how to get him away from the women and children so they could annihilate the monster before it had a chance to hurt any of them.

Tim tried to keep a neutral look on his face as he searched for a solution.

"Scott, I could use one of those," he said, nodding to the bottle of scotch. "Where's the glasses?"

"In the kitchen by the,"

"Seriously, dude, you're the host and you're supposed to take care of me."

He met his brother's eyes and hoped he was expressing his need to get him alone. "At least show me where they are."

Scott's face, which had been relaxed and happy suddenly went blank. "Sure, this way."

The two men walked into the kitchen and Tim immediately grabbed Scott's arm.

"That's the shifter, Rufus is dead." His whisper was louder than he intended and filled with anxiety.

"Son of a bitch. I got your message and thought you were just going to tell me he was on his way here, so I never bothered to call you back, because he already was."

"He must have come here straight from the kill. We have to get him out of the house and away from the others."

"But, how?"

"I'm working on it," Tim said. "You have your knife? Your gun?"

"No, they are in my lockbox under the bed."

"Go get them both and I'll get the glasses, where the hell are they, anyway?"

Scott pointed to one of the cupboards and hurried off to his room.

"Is everything alright?" Annie asked, as she stepped inside the kitchen. "You seem a little tense."

"I'm fine, it's just been a long day already."

"Where's Scott?"

"He ran into his room for something, why?"

"Just curious."

Tim didn't want her to know that Jason was sitting in the Great Room and was wearing Rufus, he was afraid it would freak her out and she would give away their element of surprise.

"Got 'em," Scott said, as he turned the corner into the kitchen, adjusting the back of shirt to cover the gun in his waistband.

"Oh," he said, stopping suddenly when he saw Annie. "Did you want a drink, too?"

"No, I'm good." She started to smile, but it faded immediately when Callie stepped out from behind him and began to growl in her direction.

Tim and Scott looked at each other and Annie quickly turned and made her way back to the Great Room.

"Callie must be able to smell him on Annie, better put her back in your room for now. We can't have her creating a scene."

"Right," Scott said, then grabbed her collar, led her back into his bedroom and shut the door securely behind him.

"Just follow my lead," he said, when he returned. The two of them headed back into the Great Room and set a half dozen glasses down on the end table.

"Who's ready for one?" Scott asked, looking around the room and shaking his head in the negative when Collin raised his hand.

"If I can't have a drink, can I at least put a movie in?"

"Not in here, we're visiting. Grab a movie and take it up to your room if you want. Shelly, you can go with them, you don't have to hang out with us boring, old people."

She turned to him with narrowed eyes. "Are you trying to get rid of me?"

"Not at all, just giving you an out, if you want one."

"I'm fine."

"Good," he said, hoping his face didn't show the frustration he felt because he hadn't been able to get her safely out the room.

"So, Rufus, you going to stay for dinner?"

"That's real hospitable of you, Scott. I'd like that. Got no family of my own."

"If I recall correctly, ribs are your absolute favorite, aren't they, Rufus?"

The man hesitated for a moment, as if searching his memory for the correct answer, then he nodded.

"Want to do me a favor, Emma, and run into town to pick up some ribs, BBQ sauce, and whatever else you'd like to go with them. The grill is the garage and I can crank that baby up in no time."

"You really want me to go to the store now?"

"Don't be silly," Rufus said. "There's no need for that."

Scott tilted his head and opened his dark brown eyes wide as he pleaded wordlessly with his wife.

"Fine," she agreed, although she didn't sound happy about it. "Are you at least going to watch Brian for me?"

"Sure, we will," Rufus said, extending his hands to take the baby from her.

A slight movement caught Emma's eye as she stood up and she saw the faintest shake of Scott's head. She also noticed that his lips were tightly pursed, as if he wanted to say something, but couldn't.

It was then that Emma felt the hair on her arms rise in alarm and knew something was very wrong. She didn't know what, but she trusted Scott and her own instincts enough to know they were all in danger.

She pulled the baby in close to her chest and walked away, leaving Rufus empty handed.

"Annie, Shelly, come on, we'll all make the trip and that way it'll be more fun. Thanks, anyway, Rufus, but Brian will be ready to eat before we get back, so it's best if he comes with us, after all. Bundle up girls, let's hit the road."

Annie seemed hesitant, but Emma was firm. "I'm not going alone and I'm not taking no for an answer. Come along, Annie, we'll be back before you know it."

Rufus no longer looked amiable, in fact he seemed downright suspicious as the women got ready to leave. Scott handed him a shot of scotch and sat down on the recliner near the couch.

"Don't worry about them," he said. "Although they probably won't be back till close to dinnertime. The shops are open and Christmas is just a few days away so I'm sure they'll find something to shop for."

After lifting his glass towards Rufus in a salute, he smiled and took a sip of the scotch. "This is good shit, by the way, thanks."

"You're welcome," Rufus replied through tight lips.

"How long you in town for?" Tim asked.

"I'll be leaving tonight."

"What's your case about, anyway?"

"It's done now, nothing left to talk about." He slowly sipped the amber liquid, his eyes darting back and forth between the brothers. He could sense their tension and knew something was not right.

"I have an idea," Scott said, standing up and moving over in front of the fire, closer to where Rufus was sitting.

"What's that?" Tim asked.

"Since everyone's gone, let's head outside and take a spin on the snowmobiles. You up for that Rufus?"

"Yeah, I don't think so," he replied, letting his eyes slide from Scott over to Tim, who was slowly moving behind the couch that he was sitting on.

"As a matter of fact," he said, standing up and moving more into the middle of the room, "I probably should hit the road. Guess I'll have to pass on the ribs this time."

He set his glass down on the coffee table and turned towards the doorway, but Tim stepped directly in front of him.

Their eyes met and both of them knew what the score was.

"I don't think so, Jason, or whoever the hell you really are. Game's up and your days are done."

It was then that Tim noticed Rufus' brown eyes were more alive than when he was, they were now golden and animal-like and were staring at him with an intense hatred. They narrowed and Tim knew he was about to make a run for it.

Before the creature could even take one full step, Tim launched himself at it, and grunted in pain as they both landed on the heavy wooden coffee table. Rufus rolled away first and jumped up, Tim grabbed at his leg, pulling him backwards.

Rufus's body was old, but the creature inside was stronger than Tim had imagined and kicked him in the ribs so hard that his body actually lifted off the ground.

Rufus turned away again, and Tim swept his leg out and tripped him. The room was large but packed with heavy furniture and this time Rufus fell forward and his head hit the arm of one of the chairs.

Tim took advantage of the moment and leapt up and twisted its arm back, placing his knee in the middle of its back to hold it down.

"Little help, Scott. What are you doing?"

Scott had kept on eye on the fight, but he was also looking for something to tie up the creature. They would kill it, but he obviously couldn't do that here in the Good Room.

"We have to finish this outside. I'm looking for something to tie him up with."

The two brothers stopped and turned towards the doorway when Collin walked into the room. "What's all the noise?"

His voice trailed off as he stared at Tim holding Rufus down onto the floor.

"Collin, you have to get back upstairs. I'll explain everything, but right now you need to get out of here and let us take care of this."

"Now, Collin," he said, a little more sharply, when the young man stood frozen in place.

Blinking rapidly, he looked over at Scott and back to Tim and Rufus then, without another word, he walked out of the room.

Tim's eyes widened when he saw Rufus' fingers growing longer and sharpening into claws.

"He's changing, come on, Scott, get over here."

All Scott could find was an extra strand of Christmas lights in a leftover box along the far wall. He grabbed it and, between he and Tim, they were able to wrap each of Rufus' hands and then they drew the wire around his waist, hoping that would keep him immobilized.

Once secured, they heaved him up onto his feet and dragged him towards the front door. The creature was strong and fought them every step of the way but, between the two of them they gradually got him closer and closer to the door.

Scott yanked it open and hurried outside. Tim followed, pushing Rufus along in front of him and neither of them saw Collin and James watching wide-eyed from high up on the staircase.

"Something's wrong," Tim said. "He's not fighting anymore."

Scott stopped as he made his way down the porch steps. "Shit, he's really changing now. Hurry up."

Rufus' face was no longer recognizable. His jaw was extended forward, and sharp canine teeth were now visible as it pulled its lips back in a grimace. Dark hair was beginning to cover its face and the amber eyes glowed with a fiery bloodlust.

Tim pushed it forward and it stumbled down the steps onto the frozen ground. When it began to stand up straight again, it had gained at least an extra foot of height and before their very eyes became broader and took on the form of a large bear.

"No time to waste, Scott, do it now."

Scott had been hoping to get it further away from the house but there was no more time. He pulled out his bowie knife and raised it, but he waited too long and the creature was too fast.

It easily broke the wire holding its hands bound and stepped closer to Scott, its golden gaze filled with hatred. In a few short seconds it was close enough to swipe out with its hairy paw.

Scott raised his arm to protect his face and the claws dug deep into his skin. The knife flew out of his grasp and when he glanced over at it, Scott realized that it was out of reach and would no longer be useful.

He turned back towards the shifter, then lifted his chin and stared bravely into the creature's face, waiting for the final blow to be dealt.

The creature raised it paw slowly and with deliberation, but suddenly threw back its head and roared out in pain. Tim had leapt onto its back and buried his own knife deep into the base of the creature's neck.

It didn't die right away but flung itself around as it tried unsuccessfully to dislodge the blade, tossing Tim to the ground in the process. Its roars of pain and anger slowly subsided and, with one last hateful look at Tim, it slid down onto the ground and released its final breath.

Scott nudged it with his boot, but it didn't respond and both men felt fairly certain it was dead.

Scott looked around and saw both Collin and James standing in the doorway, the blood had drained from their faces and their eyes were wide as saucers as they stared in disbelief at the bizarre scene in front of them.

"Damn," Scott murmured, as he walked up the porch steps. "Guys, I will explain all of this to you, but we have to finish taking care of it before your mom gets back. Will you do me a favor?"

"Are you okay?" he asked, as they just stared at him mutely.

"Yeah," Collin finally replied.

"It's important that neither your mom, nor Annie, know about this just yet, so we need to get it out of here. Would you two go clean up the Good Room? Make sure the furniture is back in place and the broken glasses picked up, put it back the way it should be. Okay?"

"Yeah," Collin repeated, finally dragging his eyes away from the dead creature and turning back into the house. James wordlessly followed along behind him.

"What now?" Tim asked.

"Got a machete in the truck?"

"Yeah, why?"

"I think it's dead, but I don't want to take any chances. Let's lop off its head just to be sure."

Tim ran to the back of his truck and got the weapon. "You don't want to do it right here, do you?"

"Not really, but what choice do we have? Help me drag it over behind the vehicles, the blood won't be so noticeable there. I'll run in and get some garbage bags to put under it. Can't have the dogs rolling in the bloody snow."

"Get my coat while you're in there and I'll head out to the ravine with it after we finish this."

They had both parts of the creature secured in the back of the truck a short time later.

Scott was just putting his phone away as Tim got into the driver's seat.

"What did they say?" Tim asked.

"I talked to Polly and they do want the creature. They've got a full lab set up and running now. They've worked on one other shifter and got some interesting DNA info. They are hoping this one might provide them with even more."

"It would help a lot if we could figure out how these things get started. It was pretty unnerving to find out how convincing they can be when they take on a human's form. If I hadn't found Rufus' body, I would never have known that was the shifter."

Scott shuddered to think of what might have happened to his family if Tim had not been able to warn them.

"They're just a couple of hours away so I'm going to head out now, but what do I do with Rufus' real body?"

"They want that, too. They want to compare the DNA of the real one and what's in the creature."

"I'm not sure I'm okay with that. Rufus deserves a proper burial."

"Come on, Tim, you know Polly and Nathan. They'll make sure he is taken care of, they've been friends with him even longer than we have."

"They better," he replied. "Do me a favor, don't talk to Annie about this. I'll come over tomorrow morning and explain everything."

"You afraid she'll take off on you once she knows it's no longer a threat."

Tim pursed his lips and rubbed his forehead. "She just might, so I want to be sure I'm the one to tell her."

"Will do but, be here early. Emma's boys know and I'm not sure they can hold their tongue. And I will be telling Emma what happened."

"I expected that. See you in the morning."

Tim jumped up into the pickup truck and was gone within a couple of minutes, leaving Scott to have his heart to heart conversation with James and Collin.

CHAPTER 17

Scott brought the boys out into the kitchen to talk with them, he grabbed a beer and tossed them both a soda. Hearing Callie whining in the other part of the house, he let her loose to come and join them.

She couldn't be bothered with the men, however, and made her way around the entire house, sniffing constantly with the hair on the back of her neck raised, particularly when she got a whiff of the Great Room.

"What was that?" Collin asked.

He was only sixteen and Scott remembered him as he'd first met him several years before. The boy had been a chubby teenager, but now he'd filled out and was a strong, handsome young man.

His voice was deeper and the only thing that Scott found unpalatable was that both he and James, with their dark hair and blue eyes, looked exactly like their father, Jeremy, which he could have done without. Fortunately, they didn't seem to share his arrogant attitude, not yet, anyway. And they never would, if Scott had anything to say about it.

Scott blew out a deep breath as he tried to find the right words to explain.

"You know there are ghosts and demons, right?"

"Of course," James replied.

"We lived with them," Collin added.

"I know, but there are other creatures out there, as well. Not just ghosts."

"Like this thing?"

"Yes, this was a shape-shifter. It's a creature that can change into other animals or even people. He took the form of our friend Rufus to get access to the house."

"Why?"

"We hunt shifters and the other creatures that are out there. Tim was helping Rufus to hunt this one and I think that's what drew it here."

He could see both boys concentrating, trying to wrap their heads around this little nugget of information.

"What other kinds of monsters are there?"

"You read my mom's books, right? The Preternatural series?"

"We've read them all, we love them."

Scott hesitated, not sure how much information he should share, they were young still and some things were best left unsaid.

"Someday, when you are older, I'll go through that series of books with you and let you know which of those creatures are real."

"Why not now?"

"Because," he hesitated and tilted his head when he thought he heard something. "Shit, I think the girls are back. Listen, this is very, very important. I will tell your mom what happened, but we can't say anything in front of Annie."

"Why?"

"Tim wants to explain it to her himself."

"Why?"

"Because."

"You say that a lot."

Scott met Collin's eyes. "There are things that its best you don't know, so will you give me a break and do as I ask, please?"

Collin looked away and nodded his head.

"Say it out loud."

"I won't say anything in front of Annie."

"And you?"

James flushed, then followed his brother's lead. "I won't say anything to her, either."

They still didn't know Scott all that well, but they were sufficiently intimidated by him that they would be sure to follow through on anything that he asked.

It was only moments later that Emma, Shelly and Annie made their way into the kitchen from the breezeway. Shelly was lugging the baby carrier and Brian was fast asleep in it.

Emma and Annie were both carrying multiple bags, some loaded with food, others with little gifts that had caught their attention while they were in town.

Scott leaned down, kissed Emma on the forehead and relieved her of the heavy bags.

"Thanks for doing this, but we might have to hold off on the barbecue, after all."

"Why?" Emma asked, she was still dying of curiosity about why he'd sent them away to begin with, but the feeling of danger was gone now, so she assumed he and Tim must have dealt with whatever it was.

"Tim and Rufus took off. Polly called and they caught another case nearby. They were going to go check it out together."

He glanced over at Annie when he heard her sharp intake of breath.

"Is something wrong?"

"No," she replied, avoiding his eyes by lowering her own towards the floor. "When will they be back?"

"Tim said he'd come over first thing tomorrow morning."

"Hey, Callie," Emma said, then frowned as she stared down at the dog.

"What is up with you lately?" she asked, as Callie continued growling. "Come on, outside until you find your manners again."

After closing the door behind the dog, she turned towards Annie. "I do apologize, there is something about you that she doesn't seem to like. Please don't be afraid of her though."

"I'm not," Annie replied, her eyes narrowed as she stared at the closed door. "I'm going to my room now, don't worry about dinner for me, I'm not hungry."

With one last sidelong glance at Scott, she made her way out to the staircase, stopping only briefly for a long look into the Great Room.

"So, what is the deal?" Emma asked.

Scott brushed a strand of blonde hair back off of her face.

"Let's get this stuff put away and head into our living room."

"Not the Great Room?"

"No, it's just us."

Emma grabbed the bags with the gifts and headed that way. Shelly followed along, carrying her little brother, who she rarely let out of her sight lately.

Scott and the boys hastily unpacked the bags of groceries and stuffed them willy-nilly into the cupboards and refrigerator, then quickly followed them.

"Spill it," Emma demanded, once they were all settled in the small, comfortable room.

"Shelly, this will probably be the biggest shock for you but, the man that was here, Rufus, wasn't actually our friend Rufus."

Emma eyebrows raised in surprised concern and Shelly shook her head and exhaled loudly.

"What kind of monster was it this time?"

"It was a shape-shifter."

"It was Annie's shape-shifter?" Emma asked.

"Yes, and before you ask, Shelly, a shifter is a creature that can change into an animal or a person."

"We watched it turn into a bear," James said, his eyes wide and his voice cracking with excitement.

"What?" Emma asked, her eyes sliding from James to Scott and her face looking rather like a storm cloud.

"In all fairness, I told them to stay upstairs, but they wouldn't listen to me."

"Just explain what happened."

"Once we finally got all of you out of danger, we had to get rid of it. There was a scuffle." He stopped talking when Collin and James smirked.

"Maybe a bit more than just a scuffle, but regardless, we got it outside and it started to change, it did look like a bear by the time we killed it."

He shrugged his shoulders as if it was no big deal.

"Holy shit," Shelly said, lifting her little brother out his carrier when he opened his eyes and began to fuss a little.

"Shouldn't we let Annie know she's safe now?"

"Tim asked us not to say anything in front of her. He'll be back in the morning and wants to explain everything to her himself."

"What does she have to do with it?" James asked.

Scott looked over at Emma, he didn't know how much to share with her children and wanted to make sure they were both on the same page.

She nodded reassuringly to him, and he said, "Before he was Rufus, he was a guy named Jason. Annie knew Jason, and actually dated him for awhile until she found out he was a shifter. She's been staying here because it was safer for her. I think he may actually have been here looking for her."

"So, you lied to us earlier about why he came here?" Collin asked, rather indignantly.

"Yes, yes, I did," Scott acknowledged. "And I'll lie to you whenever I have to, if I do it because I need to protect you, or someone else."

Emma frowned, not sure if that was necessary, but it was Scott being Scott, so she didn't say anything.

"I'm just asking all of you to please not talk about this anymore until after Tim tells Annie. The walls are pretty thin, particularly upstairs, and I don't want her to overhear anything. Agreed?"

"Agreed," they all repeated, going around the room, one after the other.

"Scott," Emma said, her voice filled with worry, "there is blood on your sleeve."

"Right," he said, pulling up the flannel material and exposing two long tears in the skin. "I better go clean that up."

"Won't you need stitches?"

He took a closer look and shook his head. "No, I don't think so."

"Was it the shifter?" James asked.

"Yes, it was, and it could have been much worse. Next time I tell you to do something, I expect you to do it. Had we not been able to subdue that monster, he would have killed Tim and me, and because you plopped your asses down to watch, you could have been hurt or killed, too. This is not a game that we play, this is real life and death shit. Don't ever disregard what I say again."

His voice was low and calm, but James shivered at the thought of what could have happened and neither of them had any intention of ignoring his directions in the future.

Tim got very little sleep that night but plied himself with some very strong coffee and headed over to Scott and Emma's early the next morning.

He walked in through the back door and found the two of them sitting in the kitchen nook. Emma was rocking a sleeping Brian in her arms and she put her finger to her lips as a way of asking him to keep as quiet as possible.

He walked over to the coffeemaker and poured himself yet another mug of coffee and then sat down beside them.

"How are you, girl?" Callie was relaxing under the table and he scratched her behind the ears before taking up the mug with both hands.

"Is Annie up yet?"

"I haven't seen her," Scott replied.

"She doesn't know, right?"

"Know what?" Annie asked quietly, as she stepped into the kitchen from the front of the house.

"We have to talk," Tim said.

She watched the little group suspiciously and did not approach any closer. Callie had gotten up quickly and was poised in a protective stance between her and the family sitting at the table.

"Scott," Emma said, indicating her head towards the dog, "maybe you should put her in our room for now."

Surprisingly, Callie tried to pull free from his grasp on her collar as he walked her out of the room in the opposite direction from where Annie stood. His eyes met Emma's and they both realized, once again, that something had to be very off about Annie for Callie to respond to her like she had been.

When he finally managed to get her out of the kitchen, Annie slowly approached.

"Would you like some coffee? A Danish?" Emma asked.

"I can get myself a cup of coffee, thanks," she said, as she went over and helped herself before sitting down next to Tim.

"What's going on?"

Tim took her hand in his. "We actually have good news, but I wanted to be here to tell you myself. Jason is dead, you don't have to be afraid anymore."

Scott walked back into the room just then. He'd heard what Tim said and was surprised at Annie's response to the news. Her eyes narrowed as she stared at Tim and her lips were pursed, almost as if she were angry rather than relieved.

But her voice was as calm and unassertive as it always was, when she asked, "How and when did that happen?"

"The man that came here yesterday, Rufus, that was actually Jason."

"How could that be?"

"Remember what we told you about shifters? He killed the real Rufus and that's how he was able to transform himself to look just like him."

"How do you know that?"

"I found the real Rufus before I came here." He still held her hand in both of his and stared down at it, twirling his thumb absently around the soft skin on her hand. "And he was dead."

She pulled her hand out of his grasp, Tim assumed she was just trying to process what she was being told, but to Scott's discerning eye, it looked like she couldn't bear the thought of him touching her.

His spidey sense was really tingling and Scott could feel his body tensing up as he tried to figure out what was really going on with Annie.

"Where is he now?"

"He's been properly disposed of."

"Buried somewhere?"

"Not exactly."

"Well, what exactly did you do with him?" she asked, and now her tone was much sharper and direct.

"I took him to some friends of ours that collect information on creatures."

"They are going to cut him up and do research? Are you serious?"

"I guess I'm a little surprised right now, Annie. I thought you would be relieved. Why are you so angry that he's dead?"

Scott watched as Annie deliberately tried to calm her features. She stared down at her cup of coffee and took a little sip before raising her eyes to Tim's once again.

"I don't know how to respond or how to react. I still can't believe that someone I cared for was a monster, a killer. It's hard to feel relieved when I know there must be more out there somewhere."

"You can't dwell on that," Emma said. "You should let this go and appreciate that you can have your life back now."

Her own feelings towards Annie were ambivalent. On the one hand she understood the confusion that was overwhelming Annie but, on the other, she also felt the woman was not, and probably never had been, completely honest with them for some reason.

"Can I?" Annie asked. "I've most likely lost my job and I don't think I'll ever be able to trust anyone again. Exactly what kind of life is that?"

"You can trust us," Tim said. "Do you want to stay here a little longer, until you can fully come to grips with all this?"

"I'm not sure," she replied.

Scott's eyes met Emma's, she could see the muscle twitching in his jaw and knew he was pissed that Tim made that offer. She wasn't exactly happy about it herself.

"Finish up your coffee," Tim said. "You and I can take a walk and talk things out, if you'd like. It's a nice, crisp morning and it'll help clear both of our heads."

"I'd like that," she replied. "Let me go get my coat and boots."

Once she was out of earshot Scott looked over at Tim with angry sparks shooting from his eyes. "What the hell, dude? Why did you tell her she could stay?"

"I'll pay you for the freaking room, Scott, if that's your problem. She's very fragile right now and can use some friends. Why do you always try to find something wrong with her?"

"Because there is always something wrong with her. Something is off, Tim, and you would realize that, too, if you'd just pull your head out of your ass and be honest with yourself."

Tim smiled and stood up, grabbed his coat off the coat rack and turned towards his brother.

"I remember saying some very similar things to you, back when we first started to help Emma out with her haunting. You totally ignored me and I'm glad that you did, because it brought us to this place right now.

In honor of that, I'm going to totally ignore you, and play this the way that feels right to me. You are just going to have to understand and accept it."

Scott ran his fingers roughly through his thick hair and shook his head. Unless he found some hard proof that Annie was something other than what she said she was, he wasn't going to be able to change his brother's mind about her, that much was obvious.

Annie returned just then, felt the tension in the room and looked at Tim curiously. He smiled tenderly and opened the door for her.

"What the hell are we going to do about that?" Scott asked, staring at the door which was now shut tightly behind them.

"I don't know, have you come to any other conclusion about what could be wrong with Annie?"

"No, I haven't, and without something concrete one way or the other, Tim's going to do what Tim's going to do."

"Did you ever ask Rufus to look into her past?"

Scott shook his head. "No, everything's been happening so fast lately that I never did ask him. We're so close to Christmas now that, if she's still here after that, I'll follow up on it myself."

"Do you think she might leave on her own?"

"Annie sure as hell seemed a lot more angry than relieved when she found out the shifter was dead, which concerns me a great deal. I have no idea why Tim is so enamored with her, but I don't think she feels the same about him. He's being taken for a ride and she may very well take off soon."

"I tend to agree with you about that, but I honestly can't figure her out. I've never had this kind of reaction to anyone before. Do you think she really could be a bona fide sociopath? Or something even more monstrous than that?"

"Hard to say," Scott replied, staring out the window of the back door, watching them walk off into the snow-covered woods.

"This type of situation is normally something that Tim and I would hash out between us to get to the truth but that, obviously, isn't going to happen this time. Maybe I'll call Nathan later on and see if he has any thoughts on the situation."

Brian woke up just then and wasted no time letting his parents know where he felt their attention should be focused, and their concerns about Annie fell by the wayside for the time being.

CHAPTER 18

Tim and Annie made their way slowly along the groomed path. The air had a frigid chill to it, but they were both dressed warmly enough that it was a pleasant stroll through the woods.

"Talk to me, Annie, why are you upset about Jason's death?"

"I already told you why. I cared about him and to find out that he was murdered just freaks me out a little."

"He was not murdered."

"What would you call it then? Was it you that killed him, or your brother?"

"I did, just as he was about to attack Scott, and after I'd seen the mangled body of a close friend that it had killed earlier. It wasn't murder and the creature had to be put down like any other rabid animal. Maybe if you would allow yourself to understand what he really was, you could accept what happened a little easier."

"I don't know," she replied, staring at the white ground in front of them, unwilling to look him in the eye. "A man that I cared about was some kind of creature and now you, another man that I care about, turns out to be a killer. I just don't know how to think or feel right now."

"I'm sorry that you think of me as a killer. If that's the case, maybe you should head back to your own home now, so you don't have to be around me any longer."

She could hear the pain and disappointment in his voice and didn't want to sever their relationship completely, at least not yet.

Annie stop walking and turned towards him, their eyes met, both similar in color but the green in her hazel eyes was glittering from the brightness of the snow.

"But I do care for you, Tim. I truly do and I'm not ready to walk away."

He pushed her oversized hood back and leaned down, taking her soft lips with his own, and she responded with a low moan and leaned against his hard body.

Pulling back away from her, he said, "I care about you, too, and I don't want you to think of me like that. What do I need to do to show you this was not anything that could have been avoided? That creature had to die so it wouldn't continue to kill people. And I was honest with you about what had to happen all along."

"You're right, but the reality was jarring, to say the least," she replied, running her mittened hand along his strong jawline. "Can you be patient with me while I try to come to grips with all this?"

"I can definitely do that. Will you stay here for a little longer then? That way, we can talk it out more if you'd like."

She stood on her tiptoes and kissed his cheek. "As long as Emma and Scott don't mind, I would like to stay until I figure out what my next best move is."

"They won't mind." Tim knew that was not exactly the truth, but he wasn't ready to let Annie go just yet. In addition to his own personal feelings, Christmas Eve was the following day and it wouldn't be right to send her off on her own just now. He knew that not even Scott could be that harsh.

"Seriously, can't you tell us?" Collin asked.

Scott stood up straight, wrench in hand, as he stepped away from the snowmobile that he was working on.

"I thought you guys wanted me to take a look at this sled that keeps cutting out."

"We do," James said, "but we also wanted to get you away from Mom, so you can talk to us for real."

Scott tried to hide his smile. "What do you mean?"

"She worries too much," Collin said, his dark blue eyes meeting Scott's, and it made Scott realize how close to adulthood the two of them were, particularly Collin.

"We know now that monsters are real, but you can't just tell us that and not explain more. Are vampires real, werewolves, what's real and what isn't?"

Scott was silent for a moment as he looked back and forth between the two of them, thinking back to what he had said to Brian about needing to know this information for his own safety.

"Please?"

"I will give you some information, not a lot. And don't roll your eyes at me, that won't help a bit."

"But how can just a little bit of info help?"

"I'll tell you what I think you need to know, and the first thing is not only the most important, but the most difficult to carry through on."

Both boy's eyes widened in anticipation of learning some great secret about a part of the world they knew nothing about.

"Before I know how much I can share with you, I have to learn how much I can trust you."

Their faces scrunched in confusion.

"If you shoot your mouths off to everyone you know about these things, you will end up in a straight-jacket, in the looney bin. There is a reason we keep these things to ourselves, that's because the majority of people will never believe you and I'm not kidding when I tell you they'll lock you up for it."

He glanced back and forth between the boys. "Can I trust you completely? Will you be able to keep your traps shut?"

The two boys nodded slowly, but Scott wasn't fooled. "We will have to take this a little at a time. If you do feel like you need to discuss any of it, come to me, or to my brother, but do not get your friends involved, understood?"

They nodded again.

"For today, we will talk about the shifters and what you witnessed. Gradually we can cover other creatures, but you're going to have to prove yourselves first."

He frowned and pulled his phone out. "Hold on, I have to take this."

Scott listened for a moment and then smiled. "That's great, I didn't think it would get here in time. It's Christmas Eve, what time do you close?"

"Excellent, I'll be there shortly."

Once he hung up, he looked over at the boys. "Sorry, I have to run into town."

He tried not to smile at their crestfallen looks. "You'll be here for a few more weeks, we have lots of time to talk about things. The sled should be fine now and maybe we can spend some time learning about how to take care of them, as well."

"Sweet," James replied, "I'd like that."

"I'm going to go see if your mom wants to ride into town with me, you guys all set?"

They nodded and he headed into the house.

"Pretty please?" Scott asked, tilting his head and opening his eyes wide as he pled with Emma.

"Ugh," she said, staring out the large bay window at the landscape which was covered under a blanket of snow. Then she turned towards the appealing fire in the fireplace and finally, lifted her eyes to meet Scott's.

"Fine, but only if Shelly agrees to watch Brian. I don't want to drag him out, too."

"Excellent," Scott said, giving her a quick kiss and heading to the bottom of the stairs where he bellowed up to Shelly.

"What do you want?" she asked, frowning down at him in annoyance.

"Will you do us a huge favor?"

"What?" Now her tone was more suspicious than annoyed.

"Will you watch your baby brother for half an hour or so while your mom and I run into town?"

She started to make her way down the stairs, wondering if she should throw some terms out so she could get something out of this, a little tit for tat, although she would never say no to spending time with Brian.

"Where are you going?"

"I ordered a black powder gun and all the accessories for Tim as a Christmas gift. I didn't think it would make it in time, but it's here and we have to run over to Lowerys to pick it up. It won't take us long."

"Oh, you aren't going to a real store?"

"Lowerys is a real store, they sell all kinds of weapons and ammunitions. Is there something you need?" He couldn't help grinning up at her, knowing where she was trying to go with this conversation.

"Not from there," she replied haughtily.

"Okay, great," Scott said.

"Brian's asleep in his crib but should be waking soon. Here's the baby monitor, but it would make me feel better if you actually went over into our quarters, so you'll be sure to hear him when he does wake up. Do you have any questions before we go?"

It was the first time Emma had left Brian in someone else's care when she was not somewhere in the house, and she felt a little anxious suddenly.

"For goodness sake, Mother, I think I can handle this."

"She's got it handled, Emma, let's go," Scott said, helping her on with her heavy winter coat and turning her towards the front door before she could change her mind.

Shelly kicked her feet up on the end table in the small living room on the other side of the house and started flipping through a magazine. When she got bored with that, she checked out the kitchen but nothing there interested her or cured her boredom.

Turning from the refrigerator, she heard Collin and James clomping down the hallway towards her.

"Quiet," she said. "Brian is sleeping."

"Oh, sorry," James said. "Where's Mom?"

"She and Scott ran to the gun store. What are you guys up to?"

"We're bored," Collin responded. "It's a perfect afternoon for a snowmobile ride. Want to come with?"

"I can't," Shelly said, her face falling. "I have to watch Brian. Besides, I thought Scott had to go with you?"

"Nah, there's no wolf out there, it was just the shifter and its dead, so we're okay to go alone."

"Would you wait a little while, until Mom gets back? Then I could go with you."

"No, it's supposed to get crappy again soon and we want to get a long ride in before the weather gets bad."

"Alright, well, maybe I'll try and catch up with you later, after they get back." Her face was the picture of disappointment.

"You can go," Annie said, startling all of them. She'd entered the kitchen so quietly that none of them had heard her coming.

"No, I can't. I have to watch Brian."

"I can do that."

"I'm not sure about that, Mom expects me to do it." Shelly sounded hesitant, but there was a hopeful look in her blue eyes as she considered the offer.

"I worked in a daycare center and I can handle a baby for a few minutes. Go with your brothers, have some fun," she said.

"Come on, Shelly, it's alright. We made a great jump yesterday, you'll love it."

"Okay, let me grab my coat. And thanks, Annie, I appreciate it. Here's the monitor, he's sound asleep in his crib right now."

"Great, and don't worry, I'll make sure he's properly taken care of. I do have one favor to ask, you have to put the dog out or I can't watch him."

Shelly hesitated, it was really frigid out and Callie was getting old. She was no longer sure that this was such a good idea, after all.

"The dog won't let me near Brian so, if not, I guess you'll have to stay back yourself."

Shelly was torn, not sure what to do, but both her brothers started pleading with her.

"Scott and Mom will be back in a few minutes, it won't hurt Callie to stay outside until then," James said.

"Come on, Sis, it'll be fun."

"Alright, fine, I'll do it."

"You sure?" Scott asked, as he leaned into the car.

"Positive, I'm going to sit right here and listen to Christmas music while you're taking care of your gun business."

"Fine, I'll be back in a few minutes."

After he shut the door, Emma leaned her head back and closed her eyes. Brian slept pretty well overall, but her own sleep did get broken up frequently during the night and it felt good to relax and rest quietly for a few minutes. However, even the lyrics of Frosty the Snowman couldn't keep her thoughts from returning to her baby.

It felt strange not having him with her and she found she couldn't relax, after all. Pulling out her phone, she checked for any messages or texts but there were none. She considered calling Shelly, just to double-check on things, but held off doing so. Emma didn't want to give Shelly the impression that she didn't trust her.

She looked over towards the front of Lowerys, but there was no sign of Scott and now she was getting antsy. She fiddled with her phone for a few minutes, checked the weather report, the local news and then, for some reason she decided to google Annie's name and see what would come up.

Her eyes opened wide and she was afraid that she might actually pass out when a very clear picture of Annie Kincaid popped up onto the screen, just above her obituary from two years before.

Emma could literally feel the panic infusing her entire body and tried to force herself to calm down. She was just about to run into the store to grab Scott, but when she opened the door, she saw that he was making his way towards her in the crowded parking lot.

The pleased look on his face dropped away immediately when he saw how pale and frightened Emma looked and he hurried over to her.

"What's the matter?"

"Look," she said, holding her phone out to him. "She's one of them, too."

"Holy shit, how can that be?" For a moment he couldn't even think straight as he tried to process this information. "That stupid bitch at the restaurant must have lied to me about the silverware. I screwed up and I'm sorry, Emma."

"Forget about that for now, come on, let's go."

He headed out as fast as he could considering the slick roads and called Gabriel first.

"Hey, Scott, what can I do for you?"

Scott blew out a deep breath and tried to keep the panic out of his voice.

"Where are you right now?"

"I'm in the barn, I just helped the kids get the sleds gassed up. They are going to hit the trails before the next bad weather blows in."

"The boys, you mean?" Emma asked.

"No, all three of them went."

"Shelly was supposed to watch Brian." Emma couldn't hide the fearful tremor in her voice.

"She said Annie is. What's going on, what's wrong?"

"You need to get to the house and keep Brian safe, Gabriel."

"From Annie?"

"Yes, she's a shifter, we just found out and he's in there alone with her."

"What do I do about her?"

"Nothing, don't let on that you know, she might hurt you. I hate to ask you to do this. Just stay with them and watch out for Brian.

If you're around, I don't think she'll try anything. I'm calling Tim now and we'll be there in a few minutes. Don't do anything stupid, wait for us to get there."

Scott hung up and immediately called Tim, grateful that he answered right away. Emma was crying softly over in the passenger seat, but he couldn't do anything about that just now.

"What's up?" Tim asked.

"Annie's a shifter and she's alone with Brian." Scott could barely force the words out, he was filled with so much anger, at himself, at Tim, and at that freaking, lying shifter bitch.

"What are you talking about?"

"Emma and I are on our way home right now. We found an obit for Annie Kincaid from two years ago, August 2017."

"There could be more than one Annie Kincaid." Tim's voice was filled with confusion.

"There's a picture," Scott said. "It's her alright, right down to the curly brown hair. She's a shifter, Tim. Can you get over to the house? We're about ten minutes out."

"I'll get there as quick as can, but you'll be there first," Tim said. "Scott, don't you lay a finger on her until I get there, understand?"

"No promises, she's got my son." He hung up the phone and pressed his foot a little harder on the gas pedal.

CHAPTER 19

Annie had Brian all bundled up in a snowsuit and he was strapped into the baby carrier in the center of the kitchen table. He woke up hungry and whining, but she had no time to feed him right then and just shoved a binky into his mouth.

Then she hurried off to his nursery and filled up his diaper bag with as many items as she could that would be needed until she was able to find a safe place to stop, which would be a long way from here.

She knew Scott and Tim would follow her to the ends of the earth, if necessary, to get the baby back. But she wanted them to, they had to pay for what they did to Jason.

Annie and Jason had been together for decades and they'd always been so careful. They moved frequently and even got their own places, just in case a hunter managed to get onto one of their trails.

She had no respect for humans, realized they knew little about her kind and wouldn't be able to grasp the fact that she and Jason actually loved each other, that they planned on spending the rest of their lives together. It wasn't easy to find another shifter, especially one that made you come alive like Jason did for her.

It had taken every ounce of restraint that she had to hold off killing the two brothers when she heard about what they'd done to him. Annie had suspected as much before they even told her because she knew he was wearing Rufus when he showed up. And she also knew he would not have left, willingly, without her.

Annie had kept in touch with Jason all along and he knew exactly where she was staying. When the hunter had first shown up at the hospital and offered to put her up, Annie got the idea to go along with them, pretend she was something that she was not, in order to find out what their plans were and what danger they posed for Jason.

Together, she and Jason had come up with an exciting new plan for the future, which was supposed to have begun that very evening, after a brief and brutal killing spree.

Annie had been quite excited about it, thinking that, perhaps there would be no more Annie and Jason but, instead, a brand new Scott and Emma. She could get used to living out here and there would be much less danger of discovery in the country.

She did find Tim attractive and would have preferred that Jason change to his body but, unfortunately, too many people in the area already knew Emma was married to Scott.

However, there was no reason he couldn't change into Tim once in awhile when they were alone. Being a shifter certainly had its perks when it came sexual fantasies.

And then there was the baby. Shifters were able to breed successfully on occasion, but she and Jason had not been lucky enough to become parents. Brian was never on their hit list, he would have survived the carnage and become their child and would never know about his true parentage.

The only other outstanding issue was Doris, if she presented a problem, she could easily be dispatched at a later time. The same held true for Gabriel and Hannah if they became suspicious.

But none of their plans had come to fruition. Annie had lain awake most of the night, debating about whether or not she would kill them all before leaving here, but Scott and Tim were hunters. They'd managed to murder Jason and she may not survive a full frontal assault on them, either.

After much contemplation, she chose to take the baby and get him someplace they couldn't find him. She was going to have to stick around until the right moment presented itself for her to grab the baby.

When Scott and Tim came looking for Brian, as Annie knew they would, she'd be sure to make them come to her, on her terms and in the arena of her making, where she would pick them off one at time.

Annie stared down into the empty crib, envisioning the brutal deaths she would deliver to the two brothers as retribution for what they did to Jason.

The images brought her a great deal of pleasure and she allowed herself a moment to appreciate her good fortune. She hadn't expected the opportunity to snatch the baby to arise so quickly, but believed it was sign that now was the time.

Their absence only allowed her a slight window of time to make her escape, but that would be more than enough to get the baby out of here before they returned and discovered what had happened.

Shaking herself out of her reverie, Annie zipped up the diaper bag and glanced around the room one last time. She had enough to last a day or two and so she headed back out to the kitchen. She grabbed the keys for Emma's mustang off the key rack and turned towards the table, stopping in her tracks as pure fury filled every inch of her body.

The baby carrier was still in the center of it, rocking slightly, but Brian was gone. Annie's jaw was clenched and she balled her hands into fists as she looked around the kitchen but, obviously, no one was there so she headed down the hallway.

She checked out each room along the way but could not find Brian or his rescuer. She was angry and frustrated and tossed furniture out of her way, taking particular delight in smashing the numerous poinsettia plants by throwing them against the walls, watching the dirt and broken plant stems dribble down onto the floor.

There was no one on the first floor. She started to open the front door, to see if they might have escaped that way, but stopped because Callie was on the porch right outside the door. Annie only opened it a sliver and was still only barely able to close it securely before Callie had a chance to force her way in.

Annie glared up the stairs, whoever it was must be up there and she would find them and kill them. She went through each room, tossing beds, tearing open closet doors, and her fury increased exponentially as she came up empty in room after room.

Annie trashed each room on the second floor and came up empty. She was fuming in the sitting area when a noise downstairs interrupted her thoughts and she walked over to the top step and looked down.

Annie bared her teeth and hissed when she saw Emma standing in the foyer and realized that her plans had gone completely awry.

Scott had parked inside the garage, hoping they could sneak in the through the breezeway without Annie noticing until it was too late. But Emma couldn't wait for him to get his weapons and went inside alone.

She saw the empty baby carrier in the kitchen and followed the destruction towards the front of the house. She heard a floorboard creak and looked up to find Annie standing on the landing.

"Where's my son?"

"How would I know?" Annie could tell that Emma knew something. She wasn't sure if she knew the entire truth, but suspected that she might.

"I'll kill you, Annie, if you touch a hair on his head."

"I haven't hurt him, why ever would I do that?" she asked with a smirk. Her shy, pleasant persona was completely gone now, as she let her real self shine through.

"Imagine my surprise when someone snatched him away from me, right under my nose. Kind of pissed me off as you can see from the state of your house."

"Why would you want to take my son?" Emma asked, she could see Scott approaching down the hall out of the corner of her eye, but Annie wouldn't be able to see him from where she was at the top of the stairs.

"We've been kind to you, we've opened our home to you. Why would you repay us that way?"

"You are a sanctimonious bitch," Annie said, her eyes narrowing. "I could barely stand being around you and your fucking Brady bunch."

Her voice got high and mocking as she continued. "Don't we all just love one another and have such a happy family."

"You're a monster, Annie, and I don't think you can fully appreciate what a real family is," Emma said, trying to keep her talking while Scott figured out what to do next.

Annie's tone was much colder and almost monotone when she replied.

"You know nothing about me and have no idea the amount of pain that your husband and his brother have caused me. They took away my family, the only thing that I have ever loved in my life and then they gave him to someone to use for research.

He's being cut up into little pieces and put under a microscope, as we speak. And you call us monsters."

Emma's eyes widened as she watched Annie's fingers lengthen and long, sharp nails began to extend out the tips of them.

"She's changing," Emma muttered, but Scott was close enough to hear and decided it was now or never.

He pushed Emma back, out of the way, and started up the steps, but stopped when the front door opened behind him. Tim's large frame filled the doorway as he looked at the small group and tried to discern what exactly was happening.

With a sharp bark and a low growl, Callie snaked her way around him and leapt up onto the stairs. She took them two at time, ignoring the pain in her hips as she finally reached the threat that she had been trying to warn them about all along.

The dog jumped up onto Annie and knocked her back on the landing. Annie held up her arm to block her face and Callie grabbed hold off it and shook her head viciously.

Annie yelled and her face began to change, her teeth lengthened, as did her jawbone, and she leaned forward and bit deep into Callie's shoulder.

The dog yelped in pain and stepped back, just as Tim reached the two of them.

He had his knife out, but he also had tears in eyes. The truth was right in front of him, changing into some sort of panther or other large cat, but he could still see Annie in that face and wasn't sure he could do what had to be done.

Scott had waited down below but when he saw the doubt on his brother's face, he hurried up the steps and raised his pistol.

"No," Tim said, putting his hand out to hold Scott back. Annie could do nothing to them because she was in the midst of changing. Once that was completed, however, it would be close to impossible to handle her or keep her from running. Both men knew that, and Scott worried Tim wouldn't be able to finish her off in time.

Scott raised his gun once more, and said, "Do it now or I will."

It was the most difficult thing that Tim had ever had to do, and that was saying a lot, but he stepped forward and plunged his knife into the heart of the half-human, half feline creature in front of him.

Annie let out a scream of agony and Tim grabbed her and held her tightly in his arms until the life faded from her body. His head was bowed as tears flowed freely down his cheeks.

"Is she dead?" Emma asked, when she reached the landing.

"Yes, she is," Tim replied, his voice was coarse, and he viciously began to wipe the tears off his face.

"Are you two alright?" Emma asked.

"I'm fine," Scott said, "but Callie got hurt."

Neither of them had any idea of how to help Tim just now. Emma rested her hand on his shoulder for a moment and then walked over to check out Callie, who was whimpering in the corner, blood oozing from the deep bite on her shoulder.

After assuring herself that Callie would be alright, Emma stood and turned to Scott. Tears overflowed from her eyes and spilled down her cheeks. With a quiet desperation, she asked, "Where's our baby?"

Scott put his arm around her, and said, "I'm sure Gabriel has Brian. We'll find him, please don't worry."

He hurried over to the linen closet and grabbed an old sheet, then helped Tim gently wrap Annie in it.

"I'll do this alone," Tim said, as he lifted the bundle over his shoulder and carried it downstairs.

"Are you taking her to Polly and Nathan?"

"No, I won't do that to her. I'm going to burn her in the ravine."

There was a large ravine on their mother's property. It was a place where they had a built a funeral pyre and would use it to cremate a creature's body when necessary.

"I'll come with you, let me find my son first."

"I'd rather do it alone, if you don't mind."

Scott was very concerned about him. Tim had obviously cared a great deal for Annie, and this was not going to be something that he would be able to bounce back from very easily.

"If that's what you want."

"It is," Tim replied, not looking back as he shut the door behind him and headed over to his truck.

Emma screamed and Scott whipped out his gun when the drop-down stairway from the cupola suddenly unfolded with a horrendous clatter.

"It's just me," Gabriel said, as he made his way down the steps and then turned towards Scott and Emma. With a crooked smile, he unzipped his coat, pulled out a little bundle and handed Emma her son.

Brian began to wail, completely oblivious to the danger he had almost succumbed to, he had waited long enough for his lunch and would wait no longer. Emma started crying and kissed Gabriel on the cheek. "I owe you more than I can ever repay. Thank you."

He blushed as she hurried downstairs with Brian clutched tightly in her arms and then Scott clasped him on the shoulder.

"What she said, consider it doubled as far as I'm concerned. You saved my son, Gabriel, there are no words to tell you how grateful I am."

His face flamed an even brighter shade of red as the two men walked downstairs side by side.

"Where's Annie?" he asked, with a nervous tremor in his voice.

"She's gone and will never be back. You won't have to worry about her ever again." Scott said, his dark eyes solemn and sincere.

Not for the first time, Gabriel reflected on whether or not he should have actually taken this gig. In the short time that he'd known Scott, Emma and Tim, he'd been exposed to more monsters than he thought had even existed at this time last year. He wasn't sure his heart could take much more.

But when his own pale blue eyes met Scott's, he felt a profound sense of respect and confidence for the man standing before him, and realized there wasn't anywhere else that he wanted to be, regardless of what the future might hold.

"I guess I better get home," Gabriel said. "Hannah is doing some baking this afternoon and I told her I'd be her guinea pig for new recipes that she wants to try out."

"Tough job but someone's gotta do it, right?"

Callie slowly limped down the stairs after them and Scott watched her affectionately as she slowly made her way off to find Emma and Brian.

"Ever the protector," he said softly.

Gabriel followed his gaze and nodded. "Yeah, she is."

They were quiet for a moment, each reflecting in their own way about the events that had just occurred.

"Hey," Gabriel finally said, "it's been a little crazy today, do you guys even still want us to come over?"

Scott thought for a moment, and then said, "Yes, I think Emma will want the whole family here for Christmas Eve, especially after what could have happened today."

"But Hannah and I aren't family."

"That's where you are wrong, my friend," Scott said, with total sincerity. "You are both family now, so you'd better get used to it. We'll see you tonight."

"Yeah, okay," Gabriel said, his face still flushed a light pink color.

Scott watched him leave and then secured the door behind him. He found Emma in their bedroom, she had just finished changing and feeding Brian and was rocking him while she patted his back.

Scott moved up close to look into his perfect little face, smiling at the milk bubble escaping from his mouth.

"Gabriel is heading home and they'll be back this evening. You do still want to go ahead with the Christmas Eve festivities, don't you?"

"I really do," Emma said, rubbing Brian's back. "I'm still a bit of wreck and can't seem to get my hands to quit shaking, but I think it will help if I stay busy and focus on what's important."

"Which is?"

Emma smiled. "Family, of course, we're all safe, and we are so fortunate to be able to be together like this. It's going to be a very special evening, I think."

"I know it will." He gently ran his hand over the crown of Brian's head and then bent down to kiss Emma.

"You could probably use some help here, but I have to leave for a little bit if you don't mind. I'll be back as soon as I can."

Emma frowned. "Where are you going?"

"Tim's burning Annie's body. He asked me to leave him alone to do it, but what you said really hit home. He's my brother and I'm going to be there for him, whether he wants me to or not."

"Go," she whispered quietly, watching his strong, broad frame as he strode out of the room.

Scott managed to get to the site just as Tim was taking the body out of the back of his truck. He'd already loaded the pyre with wood, and it was ready to set on fire as soon as Annie was placed on the platform.

"What are you doing here?" Tim asked, as Scott made his way over and helped him pull out the shrouded body.

"You don't need to do this alone," Scott said. "I'll stand here quietly and won't say a word if that what's you want. I'm just going to be here. That's all."

"Thank you," Tim said, then he started to lift the body and Scott grabbed hold to help him carry it back to the pyre.

"I feel like I should say something," Tim said a few minutes later, as they stood side by side and watched the flames shoot up into the air.

"Go ahead," Scott replied.

"That's the problem, I don't know what I should say. I feel like a fool because I truly did care about her. She completely sucked me in to believing in the persona that she was playing at, and that person, was a good person."

"Maybe that was a real part of her and that's why it was so believable."

"Except that she was a monster and I don't think it was her that carried the goodness. I think that was something inherent in the DNA of the real Annie Kincaid and I probably would have liked that person a lot. But what's burning right now is not that person. It's just an evil creature, like so many others that we've burned here."

Tim reached into his pocket and pulled out the little ceramic cat that he'd been carrying around, the gift that he had intended to give to Annie later tonight. He stared at it thoughtfully for a moment, then tossed it into the fire.

Scott could see how discouraged and down-trodden Tim looked and searched for words that might make him feel a little better about what had happened.

"Annie has spent years manipulating people and she was very good at it. None of us knew, none of us could have known, so stop beating yourself up about it, Tim. I don't want to see you lose faith completely."

The pyre and body were now engulfed in flames and black smoke was drifting high up into the crisp, blue sky.

"Lose faith in what? Myself?"

"No, in everything. I enjoyed seeing you happy, seeing you share a piece of yourself with someone that you cared about. I just don't want you to go back into your shell and start hiding those feelings again."

Tim continued to stare into the flames, but a small half-smile crossed his lips as he thought about what his brother was saying.

"Sometimes," Tim finally said, "I think that I just want what you have so badly, that I can't see what's actually in front of my face. I worry that might be why I was so taken in by Annie, I wanted her to be the one.

Now, I'm going to second guess everything and everyone that comes into my life because I'm not sure I'll ever be able to trust anyone again."

"You could always stick any new potential girlfriend with a silver knife from here on out. If the silver doesn't burn them, they're good, right?"

"It's not just about shifters, Scott."

"I know, it's much bigger than that, but you gotta get back on the horse, Tim."

"You, Emma, and even Mom, knew there was something off about Annie, but I fought all three of you every step of the way. My judgment is whacked, so I think I'd better step back for a little while."

"Don't wait too long, brother. You might miss out on something important."

"Christmas miracles, right?"

"You never know."

CHAPTER 20

Emma spent the afternoon cleaning up after Annie's tirade and finishing up whatever cooking still had to be done.

Doris had come over a few hours before and after they'd explained the situation with Annie, she had been a godsend, helping with the cooking and the preparations for the evening's festivities.

"I'm glad that girl's gone," Doris shared with Emma privately. "I didn't like her from the very beginning and neither did Tolstoy."

"How's he doing anyway?"

"I had to take that horrible cone off his head, he was having a terrible time with it. He's still a little sore, but he's doing much better."

The pup had pricked up his ears at the sound of his name and hurried over to Doris' side. She rubbed his ears and then sent him on his way.

"Go find the boys, maybe they'll play ball with you."

The afternoon flew by and before they knew it, it was time for the festivities to begin and they all congregated in the Great Room.

Doris had cleaned up Callie's wound and the dog was now spending most of her time recovering on her orthopedic pillow, which they'd placed in here, as well, so she could be with the family.

Emma and Scott were standing in the arched entryway, watching all the commotion. The tree was in front of the bay window, its colorful lights blinking merrily, and there were piles and piles of gifts under the tree.

Dean Martin was crooning Christmas carols and the furniture had been moved more towards the center of the room so the long folding tables could be lined up along one wall. They were decorated with festive table clothes and groaned under the weight of all the holiday treats that rested upon them.

"Do you think Tim will show up?" Emma asked, as she watched Shelly and Doris chit-chatting on one of the couches. Shelly had finally given up possession of Brian and Emma wasn't sure that she had ever seen such a happy, relaxed look on Doris' face as when she stared down at her grandson.

"I think he will, I hope so, at least. It's a strange time for him."

The doorbell rang just then, and Scott opened the door to let in Gabriel and Hannah. They were all smiles and were lugging in bags full of gifts and food.

"Let's put these gifts under the tree, shall we?" Emma asked, trying not to giggle as she checked out Hannah's sweater, which was a pretty red with green edging around the bottom of the sleeves, the neck and along the bottom of the sweater itself.

It was the large deer head in the center of the sweater that really caught Emma's eye, she assumed it must be a reindeer but, for some obscure reason, it wore an eyepatch and had a mustache.

Scott walked up behind Emma and wrapped his arms around her, looking over her shoulder.

"Wait, not that one," Hannah said, taking the bag back from Emma.

"Gabriel will have to explain this," she said, trying not to watch Scott's hands as they continued to hold Emma securely in their gentle grip.

"Hey, Gabriel, why didn't you tell us we were having an ugly sweater contest?" Scott called out. "Even if we did know, that one would be tough to beat. And Hannah, I gotta give you a close second on yours."

Gabriel puffed his chest out proudly and everyone in the room started to chuckle. Seen from a distance it looked like he was wearing a red cardigan with fuzzy white edging, opened wide and exposing only a red tie with candy canes on it and some incredible washboard abs.

"Hannah wants me to wear it all the time," he said, and she blushed an even deeper shade of red and stared at the floor.

Completely oblivious to Hannah's discomfort, Gabriel pulled out a covered bowl and handed it to Emma.

"What's this?"

"Julegrot."

"Come again?" Scott asked.

Gabriel lifted the lid and they could see what looked like rice pudding filling the container.

"Julegrot, it's a Swedish tradition for Christmas Eve."

"Didn't you tell us you were German?"

"That's my mom's side."

"We can put that out with the other food," Emma said. "What's so special about it?"

"Before I explain the Julegrot, you need to know what a tomte is. A tomte is a mischievous sprite which protects farmsteads and their buildings, that's why I thought we should be sure to have it tonight, now that you have a farm and all."

Emma stepped out of Scott's grip and glanced up at him, pleased to see that he was enjoying the story from Gabriel.

"A tomte," Gabriel said, as the others came closer to hear his story, "looks like an old man with raggedy clothes and a bright red cap on his head. Oh, and he's only the size of a child. My mom used to say they looked a lot like those garden gnomes you see all over the place."

Gabriel's face was filled with happiness as he looked around the room and felt a part of this large, wonderful family.

"The Tomte works very hard caring for the animals and he keeps the home and the barn clean and orderly. But," Gabriel paused for dramatic effect and looked over the crowd once more before continuing, "they ask for nothing in return, other than the farmer's respect and a bowl of Julegrot, or Christmas porridge with butter on it, for Christmas Eve. If he doesn't get it, he can be quite a little devil."

"And Gabriel made me really load it up with butter so it's very rich," Hannah warned.

"I wanted to be sure it was the way the Tomte likes it," Gabriel said, then turned to Scott and Emma. "I put a little bowl out in the barn, too. I wasn't sure if that would be the right place but, if not, it's also in here if he wants it, right?"

"Oh, Gabriel, you don't really believe it exists, do you?" Hannah asked, as she rolled her pretty brown eyes.

"You'd be surprised what really does exist in this world, Hannah," he said, turning and winking at Scott in a knowing manner.

They all dispersed around the Great Room, either exploring their options along the tables loaded with goodies, or simply trying to find a spot to get comfortable.

Scott was still in the entryway, trying to hold back his laughter about Gabriel's Tomte, when the front door opened again and a gust of cold air blew into the house. Tim stepped through the door and Scott hurried over to greet him, with Emma right behind.

"I'm really glad that you came, Tim."

"Couldn't miss this," he said. "I heard the food was to die for."

He took Emma into his arms and gave her a heartfelt hug. "Merry Christmas, Emma. Before we go in with the others, I want to take a minute and make sure you know how much you and your kids mean to me, and how grateful I am that you are a part of our lives. You've shown us a whole different side of life than we ever knew before."

"Thank you," she said, tears filling her green eyes as she looked up at him. Then she took his hand and led him into the Great Room with all the others.

"Tim's here, can we do presents now?" James yelled, puffing out his lower lip in a pout and blinking his dark blue eyes at his mother.

"You are so bad," she said, then turned to Scott. "We've always allowed one present to be opened on Christmas Eve, are you agreeable to that?"

"I don't know," he replied, and both James and Collin opened their eyes wide at the thought they might not get any gifts until tomorrow. "My mom never let us do that. What do you think, Mom?"

Doris pursed her lips and blew out a long breath, then looked sternly at the two boys. "I always figured it would spoil the children. After all, making them wait for something they truly want strengthens their character."

Now the two of them were staring at Doris in horror.

"But, why not? It's our first Christmas together, let's go for it," she added with a huge smile.

"Thanks, Doris," James said, sprinting over towards the tree.

"Collin and James," Emma said, "please be sure to give one to everyone, don't just grab your own."

The two of them spent several minutes digging through the piles of presents under the tree, picking out the one that they wanted to open for themselves, and then delivered a single gift to each of the others.

Shelly had taken back possession of her baby brother from Doris and wasn't willing to give up holding him, not even for the chance to open a gift. She left hers on the floor next to her feet where James had tossed it, and just glared at him as he hurried away to tear open his own treasure.

Scott and Emma stood back, away from the mayhem, their arms wrapped around each other and Emma's head resting against his shoulder.

"Is this how you thought it would be?" Emma asked quietly.

"Never in a million years," he replied.

She stepped away from him so she could look up into his face, confused at his response. "What do you mean?"

"This is better than anything I could have imagined. I didn't know I could be this happy and can't wait to see what happens next."

Suddenly the doorbell rang and Scott and Emma's eyes met, they were not expecting anyone else. Scott was not wearing his gun but asked Emma to stay back until he could see who it was.

He looked out the peephole and turned to Emma with a look of total confusion on his face. Scott turned the handle and a young woman stepped through the door and threw off her hood, smiling brightly as she did so.

"Hi, Scott, Merry Christmas. I hope you don't mind me crashing your party, but Doris called and was pretty insistent that I come over and join in."

Emma made her way to Scott's side and extended her hand towards the statuesque beauty. "I'm Emma, Scott's wife."

"Nice to meet you, my name is Sarah Johnson. I've been kind of a friend of the family for many years."

"She was engaged to Tim," Scott said, still not sure what to make of any of this.

Then Tim stepped out into the foyer to see what was going on. He stopped short and the blood drained from his face when he realized who was standing there.

"Holy shit," he murmured, then a huge grin split his face and in just a few strides he was in front of her, engulfing her in a bearhug which she enthusiastically returned.

Scott and Emma just looked at each and smiled.

Maybe Christmas miracles really do happen.

THE END

THANK YOU

Thank you for joining me in this latest Devereaux adventure. I hope you enjoyed it.

I wrote the majority of this story during the 2020 coronavirus lockdown. Fortunately, this is a continuation of a story which began in early 2019 and ends at Christmas 2019, before the virus caused such an upheaval in our lives.

The Devereaux family will be on a bit of a hiatus for a while as I am currently working on something completely different.

Please be sure to check my website, debbieboek.com, for information on my upcoming novel, as well as all of the others that are currently available.

Take care and stay safe.

Debbie Boek
debbieboek.com

Printed in Great Britain
by Amazon

62475602R00118